To my friends and family.

Without you this book wouldn't exist.

AFTER EPILOGUE

BOOK ONE: THE ASHES

WRITTEN BY MAX HOWL

Chapbook Press

Schuler Books
2660 28th Street SE
Grand Rapids, MI 49512
(616) 942-7330
www.schulerbooks.com

After Epilogue – Book One: The Ashes

ISBN 13: 978196619242

eBook ISBN: 9781966196259

Library of Congress Control Number: 2025910773

Edited by Jessica McKelden

Printed in the United States by Chapbook Press.

Chapter One

In these lands of scorched earth and cloudless sky,
Water is scarce,
And desperation runs high.

. . .

On top of the sandstone mesa glowed a small red sphere of fire, its embers dancing with the stars. The smell of burning kindling wafted through the chill night air, the crackle of the fire's feast echoing through the quiet dunes below. Sitting cross-legged beside the fire was a woman leaning back onto the palms of her hands, soaking in its warmth. She had beautiful black skin and a shaven head, with eyes that looked through things rather than at them. A thin scar was engraved on her cheek, cutting diagonally across her ear. Gold shimmered on the buttons of her vest and the brim of her cowboy hat. A matching golden pistol sat silently in the holster at her hip.

"Damn," she cursed, staring through the hole in her canteen. She shook the last few drops of water into her mouth and sighed, dissatisfied. "That idiot managed to miss me but shot my canteen. I don't know which is worse, to be honest," she sighed.

The night stood quietly above her, a vast blanket of stars and planets. Her dark eyes reflected the moonlight like the blue sky in water.

"At least I've still got these," she groaned, taking a can of beans from her satchel. She unclipped a knife from the strap across her thigh and stabbed it into the top of the can. Clumsily, she worked it around the can's perimeter until the lid popped clean off. Using the knife as a spoon, she carefully scooped the cold beans into her mouth and chewed.

She paused as a slithering sound echoed up the side of the mesa. A sepequs climbed up over the edge with a rider upon its back. The sepequs had the appearance of a snake but was the size of a horse, fitted with a saddle and reins. This one, in particular, was rust red with white and black stripes. The sepequs's rider had toffee-brown skin, her black, curly hair pushed back by a dark-green headband. She had thick, sturdy limbs and a plump figure which she carried with an air of pride. A sleeveless white blouse was buttoned over her chest, tucked into a high, pleated skirt. Vera watched with cool contentment as the stranger drew close.

"Hello, I don't mean to intrude. I just saw your fire and was hoping to warm up a bit. You'd think a desert would be hot, but I'm near freezing," the rider said awkwardly. "My name is Emaline."

"You can call me Vera," the woman with the cowboy hat said. "Are you from the city or something?" she added with a skeptical glare.

"Is it that obvious?" Emaline chuckled, rubbing the back of her sunburnt neck.

"Most folks don't trek out here unless they know they'll be warm come nightfall,"

Emaline's eyes wandered down to the can of beans in Vera's hand, her stomach groaning loudly. She laughed and cocked an embarrassed grin. "Forgot to pack some food as well," she said sheepishly.

Vera inspected the sepequs, glaring at the bags tied to the sides of its saddle. "Whatcha got in there, then?"

Emaline reached over the side of the saddle and untied the bags, revealing two glass jugs of water.

"Stranger, you're in luck," Vera chuckled, smiling. "I have food but no water, and you have water but no food. I think we might be able to come to a compromise here."

"I'll shake to that," Emaline said, sliding off the sepequs and shaking Vera's hand.

After a few minutes, they'd managed to empty two cans of beans and half a jug of water. The women both sighed with their hands resting on their full, happy bellies. The sepequs slithered up beside Emaline, pushing its head onto her lap.

"You must be hungry, too, huh?" she teased, tossing the remains of her dinner into the sepequs's open maw.

"So, how'd you end up all the way out here?" Vera asked.

"It's not a long story. Or a very interesting one." Emaline gently petted the top of the sepequs's scaled head.

"I doubt that. You're traveling with two gallons of water. Probably four, if I opened the bags on the other side of that saddle. Besides, this isn't any ordinary well water—this is *pure*." Vera eyed the sweat growing across Emaline's face. "You must be sitting on a fortune in order to afford this kind of stuff."

"…It's true," Emaline admitted, rolling her thumbs. "I come from a very wealthy family. I've never even stepped foot in the desert before—but you already figured that out."

"So why leave?" Vera asked. "Most folks would kill—*have* killed—to be where you are, to have what you have."

Emaline turned and stared off into the desert, painted purple under the night sky. "The ashes…" she murmured.

"Ashes?"

"My father passed away about a month ago. His dying wish was that his ashes be spread in the Jungo River," Emaline explained. "Nobody else in my family wanted to go. They didn't like my father much to begin with. So I grabbed what I could and I left."

"Well, spare your family another funeral and head back," Vera said bluntly.

"I can't," Emaline protested. "This is simply something I have to do." Suddenly, her naïve, teary eyes lit with an idea. "What if *you* took me there?" she asked excitedly.

"*Huh?*" Vera gasped.

"You wouldn't go unpaid," Emaline quickly added. "I'd like to hire you to get me safely to the Jungo River." She held out a drawstring bag of bronze oreales.

"You got a death wish or something? If you were to point to Jungo on a map, you wanna know how far we are from it? We'd be on opposite corners. An inexperienced thing like you wouldn't last a day."

"But that's where you come in," Emaline explained. "You know how to survive out here. You can teach me." After realizing Vera was unmoved by her little speech, Emaline continued, "You *are* a mercenary, aren't you?"

"What gave you that impression?"

"Well, you look the part, I suppose. You've got a mysterious glare."

"Mysterious glare," Vera chuckled loudly. "Fine, then. So what if I am?" She sighed, thoroughly amused.

"Mercenaries like money," Emaline said, like it was a fact. "And I have money."

Vera shook the small drawstring bag. "A service of this stature is worth more than this."

"Think of it as a down payment. Once you get me to Jungo, I'll get in contact with my family and ensure you're well compensated."

Vera considered the idea a moment, thinking up at the stars. "Sounds like a clean deal to me," she said, holding out her hand.

Emaline stared at the gesture, a little surprised at her own negotiation skills. With a cheery smile, she reached out and shook.

Just then, as if an omen, red light stretched across the sand with the rising sun. It climbed up the mesa, lighting their faces in crimson.

Chapter Two

The sepequs's limbless body swam through the sand with ease, moving at unbelievable speed. Emaline sat at the front of the sepequs, holding the reins, while Vera sat sideways across the back. The sun they'd watched rise over the horizon had crawled to the middle of the sky, the peak of the day when it burned its hottest and brightest. Emaline could feel her skin beginning to burn and the sweat clinging to her clothes. She'd attempted to make conversation, but Vera had only responded with either a nod or a one-word answer. Eventually, Emaline gave up on trying to make small talk and instead took in the scenery around her. There was little to look at besides the sand, but occasionally, there was an acacia tree or cactus that would catch her attention.

In the distance rose a town of clay homes with hollow windows. A solar farm sat beside the town, rows of glistening metal panels that hummed softly with energy. The town was so small, so beaten by the wind, that it looked more like a product of nature than of man; something of accident rather than purposeful structure.

"Better stop for supplies," Vera said. "We ate up the last of our rations last night."

Emaline steered the sepequs toward a wooden post. She slid off the saddle and wrapped the reins around the post in a playful knot.

Walking through the town, Vera and Emaline passed by slumped figures with somber, sun-stained faces. The townspeople looked at them, not with compassion or hostility, but with mundane interest, like watching a swooping insect or a particularly strong gust of wind.

"Not a very talkative town," Emaline whispered.

"Talk leads to trouble," Vera advised. "If you take any lesson from us traveling together, I hope you learn that."

At the end of a row of homes was a long building with a sign that read *Shop* in big, red, painted letters. Inside the shop was a man sitting behind a counter, fanning himself lazily with a magazine. A dozing cat with ginger fur snored softly on the wooden counter beside him.

"We're looking for some grub—nothing that melts or rots," Vera said.

The man peered up at her and reluctantly opened his mouth to speak. "Last aisle on the right," he groaned, itching his gray stubble.

Vera tipped her hat and strutted down the metal aisles, filling her satchel with canned and dried foods. While she shopped,

Emaline stood idly at the entrance. Her eyes scanned the first aisle and lit at the sight of a sweet bun wrapped in wax paper.

"My wife made those," the man said, catching Emaline's gaze. "Made them fresh this morning."

Vera cut between them, placing her satchel onto the counter and taking out the drawstring bag Emaline had given her. "How much do I owe you?" she asked.

"I'd say…twenty," the man said, digging through the supplies in the satchel.

Vera glanced back over her shoulder and looked into Emaline's hungry eyes. "Make it twenty-two," she added, grabbing one of the honeyed buns from the shelf.

"You didn't have to do that," Emaline said as they walked out of the store.

Vera shrugged. "They were cheap, and you look hungry."

"You know what you remind me of? Those chivalrous knights from the Old Stories," Emaline said with a sway in her step.

"And what would that make you? A princess?" Vera teased.

"Back home, I pretty much was one." Emaline took an eager bite of the bun, flakes of pastry clinging to her lips. Her fingers turned white with powdered sugar, which she dusted off onto her clothes.

She's messy for a princess, Vera thought. *Not that there's anything wrong with that.*

A few feet ahead of them was an ancient brick well with a rickety wooden roof. Standing in front of the well was a man in a mesh shirt and baggy camo pants, cursing at an old woman in a shawl.

"Y-you can't have it," the old woman said sternly, her teeth chattering with anger.

"Move out of the way, Grandma," the man spat. "We're draining this well."

"If you take this, then we're as good as dead!" the old woman cried.

"I said: get out of my way!" the man snarled, shoving the old woman to the ground.

"Hey!" Emaline raced to the old woman's side and helped her up onto her feet. "Who do you think you are?" she asked, holding a finger up to the man.

"Wylie Rydes. Leader of the Golden Jackal Gang," he introduced himself. He had shaggy, dirty-blond hair pulled back into a short ponytail. A silver fang hung from his right ear, and a sharp snaggletooth peeked over his bottom lip.

"You can't just leave these people with nothing to drink," Emaline said.

Wylie smirked. "Actually, I can." He reached out and grasped Emaline's hand, holding it up to his mouth to kiss it. "A pretty thing like you shouldn't be out in this heat. I can tell you're a royal just by looking at you. The rest of my gang is currently dealing with other affairs, but I'd love for you to meet them. Why don't you come back with us? You'll be safe with me—"

Before he could finish, Emaline kicked him in the shin, forcing him to let go of her hand.

"Why, you—!" Wylie reeled back his arm as if to hit her, but then froze.

He peered back over his shoulder and found Vera clenching his wrist from behind. Enraged, he took back his hand and turned to face her, but before he could even get a word out, she had already drawn her pistol. She aimed the barrel to the right of Wylie's head, just below his ear.

Even as the sweat fell from his face, Wylie held on to a toothy sneer. "Is that supposed to be a threat? You aren't even aiming at me."

"Wasn't trying to," Vera said coolly. She pulled the trigger, a loud bang erupting from the barrel.

The bullet whizzed past Wylie's face, ricocheted off a metal sign, and nicked him in the ankle. Wylie yelped like a wounded animal, wincing. The searing pellet dug into the sand beside Wylie's bleeding foot, smoking.

Trembling, Wylie reached for his earring but only grasped at the air. In a panic, he reached a little higher and sighed with relief when he felt his ear was still there.

"You'll pay for this!" Wylie spat, limping back toward the hoverbike he had driven into town with. As he turned the key, the hoverbike rumbled to life, skidding off over the dunes.

The villagers all gathered around the well, cheering and clapping. While Vera felt slightly overwhelmed by the adoring crowd, Emaline happily soaked up the attention.

With an annoyed grumble, the shopkeeper peeked out of his store to check on the commotion, his eyes lighting up at the sight of the old woman. He raced to her, holding her face in his wrinkled hands. "Are you alright?" he asked.

"I am now," the old woman reassured. "These young ladies just saved my life—all of our lives," she explained, pointing to Vera and Emaline.

The shopkeeper looked at them differently than he had before—his eyes softer, more gentle. "Thank you," he said. "Please, tell me how I could repay this kindness?"

"There is one thing…" Emaline began with a sly smile.

A little while later, Emaline skipped to the village's outskirts with a satchel stuffed with pastries. "I knew it," she whispered playfully to Vera, bumping her hip.

"Knew what?" Vera asked.

"You've never taken a life, have you?" Emaline teased. "A pacifist mercenary. That's a little ironic, now isn't it?"

"We can reach the next town over if we get a move on," Vera grumbled, ignoring Emaline's question.

"Damn," Vera swore. She snapped the reins, but the sepequs was already moving as fast as it could.

The sky was slowly blackening, casting an encompassing shadow over the desert. The sand that had spent all day burning in the sun hissed in the cold of the coming night.

"I thought you said that we could reach town—" Emaline began.

"I know, I know," Vera grumbled. "You just had to get caught up in someone else's problem and waste good daylight."

"You expected me to just leave it be?"

"That's the best thing you can do," Vera said. "Besides, don't act like you're any more innocent than he was."

"Excuse me?" Emaline fumed.

"Remind me again where your family got that pure water from?" Vera asked. "The people in small towns like the one we just passed through…all they got are those wells. They dig into the unforgiving soil, the sun at their backs, only to strike a hand's worth of water. And that's on the good days," she explained. "They don't have the money to spend on Aquis's supply. Heck, even if they did, I doubt they'd give them any. But to the families like yours, who lounge in air-conditioned palaces, never knowing of thirst, you're always willing to toss them a penny—"

"That's enough!" Emaline yelled.

Vera pulled back on the reins, bringing the sepequs to a stop. She peered back over her shoulder at Emaline, who looked on the verge of tears.

"I may not know much about this desert, but that doesn't mean I don't know *anything*. You don't think I know what Aquis is, what they've done?" she asked, glaring at Vera. "I told you that my family didn't care about my father dying or me leaving, but do you know why? It's because we wanted something *better* for this world and for the people in it than Aquis. My father was a scientist; he knew how to do it, but he didn't *live* long enough to figure it out. And after years of work with no results, I just want to let him *rest*. That's why I have to get these ashes to Jungo, and I can do that with or without your help."

Vera cleared her throat and tipped her hat. "I'm sorry," she said, softening her tone. "Most folks can't understand what life is like out here for us."

"I don't, and I won't act as if I do." Emaline sighed. She reached out and touched Vera's hand. "But I want to try. Maybe we can learn to talk to one another…to understand one another. My father may be gone, but I won't let his research go to waste. After this is all over, I want to finish what we started."

"Do you really have hope in a world like this?" Vera asked.

"If we don't have hope, then what's left?"

Vera made a little noise, a tensing of the throat. She turned back around and went to snap the reins when suddenly, six furry legs burst out from the sand and wrapped themselves around the sepequs's body. An enormous spider began to rise up from the earth, unburying itself from the sand.

"What is that thing?" Emaline asked.

"It's a snare spider," Vera growled, pulling out her pistol and taking a shot at one of its eyes.

The spider stabbed its pincers into the neck of the sepequs, who wriggled with pain.

"No!" Emaline cried.

Vera grabbed Emaline's hand and leaped off the saddle, rolling across the cool desert sand. She turned and fired two more times, but the spider remained unfazed—for every eye it lost, there were over a dozen to replace it.

The spider dragged the sepequs's limp body down into the sand, the ground flattening above it, leaving no indication of the monster lurking beneath.

"No," Emaline panted. "That saddle had all of our supplies…all of our water…" She buried her face in her hands, collapsing onto her knees. "I shouldn't have ever come here…"

Vera stared down at her for a moment, then walked over to a nearby cactus. She took out her knife and lobbed off a piece of the cactus's flesh. "Here." Vera offered the slice of cactus, peeling off the needles like the skin of an apple. "It's good for you, and will keep you from getting dehydrated."

Emaline stared at the gift for a moment. Gently, she took it into her hands and brought it up to her mouth. She was surprised by the flavor, a tangy sweetness her tongue had never tasted.

"This desert can be cruel, but it can also provide for us," Vera explained. "It might not be the most hospitable place, but it's all we got, and we've learned to adapt to it pretty well."

Emaline finished off the slice of cactus, wiping the juice from her lips.

"I'll get you to Jungo," Vera said.

Emaline sniffed. "Really?"

"Just because this world is cruel doesn't mean I have to be. You have good intentions, even if they're a bit naïve. Besides, you're already plenty tough. I mean, you took on the leader of the Golden Jackals and walked off without so much as a scratch. You just need someone to show you the way."

"Thank you," Emaline said, standing. She wrapped her arms around Vera, who stiffened.

Vera coughed awkwardly. "It's not a big deal. I mean, you're paying me to get you there, after all."

"Of course," Emaline said more formally, pulling away.

"Wait—what about the ashes?" Vera began anxiously.

Emaline untucked a necklace from beneath her blouse collar and held up the silver vial attached to it. "I always keep them on me."

Vera cracked an impressed smile and shook her head, chuckling softly. "Without a sepequs, we'll be doing a lot of walking." She sighed, folding her hands behind her head.

"I don't mind walking," Emaline said as they began to trudge through the sand together.

Vera chuckled. "Trust me—come morning, you will."

Chapter Four

Vera was right. By the time the sun rose, Emaline was praying for nothing more than a place to sit and rest her feet.

"When we get to the next town, we'll buy you a pair of proper sand shoes," Vera said, noting Emaline's limp.

"But we don't have any money. We spent most of it, and then that spider ate the rest."

"Everybody needs something done that they aren't willing to do. Usually, they'll toss you a few oreales if you do a good enough job."

As if summoned by her words, a house began to emerge from the hazy horizon. It was built into the side of a canyon with red clay walls and a straw roof. Emaline raced for the shade, letting the shadow of the canyon wrap around her like a cool blanket. A herd of scrawny goats watched her from a wooden pen, bleating curiously. Sitting beside his livestock was a farmer with a cotton robe holding a gnarled shepherd's staff.

"We don't need more mouths to feed," the farmer spat.

"We won't stay long," Vera explained. "Just looking for some work."

"Plenty of work to be done," the farmer chuckled softly. "I'm not as spry as I once was. Makes tending to the farm more difficult than it used to be."

"We'd be happy to help. Perhaps for some food and a little water?" Emaline bargained.

"And a pair of sand shoes," Vera added.

"I think we can make that happen," the farmer said, slowly getting to his feet. "My name's Havert."

"I'm Vera, and this is Emaline," she said, shaking the farmer's hand.

Havert gave the women several tasks to complete, and they did so with eagerness. Emaline cared for the goats, combing their shiny pelts and rubbing beeswax on their sharp horns. She pruned the peach tree growing in the shade at the edge of the canyon, filling wicker baskets with its ripe harvest. Meanwhile, Vera fixed whatever was broken, tightening door hinges and hammering in loose planks in the fence. She carried heavy buckets of goats' milk to and fro, emptying them into a stone barrel. And as she worked, she found her eyes always wandering to wherever Emaline was.

"I think that's enough for today," Havert said as the sun began to set. "Come inside. I'll make you some food."

"We really can't thank you enough," Emaline said politely.

"This canyon has blessed my family for generations. The shade has protected us from the sun, allowing us to grow what few things we can," Havert explained. "We might as well share our blessing with those who've earned it."

Havert prepared each of them a bowl of roasted vegetables, goat cheese, and spiced peaches. They ate in silence, choosing not to spoil their meal with words. Once their bowls were empty and their stomachs were full, Havert retreated upstairs to his room. He had made two makeshift beds out of hay and burlap for Vera and Emaline to sleep in.

While lying on one of the makeshift beds, Emaline held up her hands toward the ceiling, staring at her calloused fingers. "He had us working from dawn to dusk," she laughed. She turned onto her side to face Vera, who had her hat tilted over her face. "Did you come from a desert town? Or was it an independent home like this one?"

"Have you ever heard about the cat that got too curious?" Vera said.

Emaline pouted. "You already know so much about me. It only feels fair that I should know a little about you. We'll be traveling together, after all."

"Don't know where I came from—no one does. I was taken in by a wandering traveler when I was young," Vera explained.

"How did you end up becoming a mercenary?"

"I thought that the traveler had taken me to heaven on earth. But it wasn't. It was gilded, and once I scraped away its golden exterior, there was nothing worth staying for. Eventually, I chose to run away and make my own way in life."

"That sounds lonely," Emaline murmured. "I wasn't very close with my family, but at least I have—*had* my father."

"Let's turn in for the night. Save our strength for tomorrow," Vera said awkwardly.

"Oh, yes," Emaline stuttered, a little crestfallen. She leaned over and blew out the flame in the lantern between them, casting the room in darkness.

. . .

Emaline couldn't identify the noise at first, but she quickly recognized the octave of fear. The goats outside were bleating pitifully, their cries piercing Emaline's dreams. She rose wearily from the bed and found that it was still dark outside. There was a loud snarl, then the sound of splintering wood. Emaline turned and shook Vera awake.

"There's something outside," she said hurriedly.

Vera grabbed her pistol and kicked open the front door, racing toward the goat pen.

Two large coyotes with glowing yellow eyes and acidic mouths were trying to break into the fence. The goats all huddled together in the corner of their pen, shivering fearfully.

Vera aimed her pistol at the sky and fired, grabbing the coyotes' attention. One of the beasts snarled, peeling back its pink lips to reveal a row of sharpened fangs eager to bite and tear. It darted toward her at full speed, kicking up a cloud of dust. Vera shot her gun, nicking the animal in the side. It whimpered and scampered off, licking at the wound. Its twin leaped up from behind and pinned Vera to the ground, her pistol slipping from her grasp and landing in the sand a few feet away. She struggled against the creature's heavy chest, shoving back its snapping jaws from her throat.

Bang.

A bullet skimmed the creature's paw and shot into the sand.

The coyote whipped its head in the direction of the gunshot and snarled. Emaline was standing nearby, her trembling fingers gripping the trigger of the golden pistol.

"I don't want to hurt you," she said. As she aimed the barrel of the gun, she noticed the coyote's frail figure, its ribs jutting out from beneath its skin. "You're just hungry, aren't you?" she said, lowering the pistol.

"What are you doing?" Vera hissed.

"No one should have to starve," Emaline said. She reached for a bundle of dried lizards tied above the door frame and tossed them to the coyote.

Hesitantly, the coyote approached the bundle and sniffed at it, gently taking it into its mouth. It darted off into the desert, its bushy tail wagging wildly.

"I can't believe that worked. You know, you're actually a pretty good aim," Vera said, standing. Her eyes fell onto Emaline, who had slumped against the doorframe with her hand on her head.

Suddenly, Emaline sprang forward and threw her arms around Vera.

"I-I thought it was going to kill you."

"Hey…it's okay," Vera said soothingly.

"I thought I would be all alone…" Emaline held back a sob.

Vera wrinkled her lips and held Emaline close, petting her kinky black hair. She reached down and took Emaline's hand into her own, pressing it against the top of her chest. Vera's steady heartbeat bounced beneath Emaline's fingers.

"See? Still alive," Vera said softly. "And it's all thanks to you."

Emaline hid her face from Vera with an embarrassed smile. "You must think I'm pretty pathetic, reacting like this."

"It's not easy to have a soft heart in a hard world," Vera said, lifting up Emaline's chin so they were face to face.

"What happened?" Havert's raspy voice called from the doorway of his cottage.

Emaline shrunk away from Vera, hurriedly unwrapping her arms.

"Just a couple of coyotes causing trouble," Vera explained. "Don't worry; we handled them."

"I see," Havert murmured. "You saved my herd, and for that, I am extremely grateful. Here, I want you to have these." He searched for something in his robe pocket, pulling out two faded tickets, and placing them in Vera's hand.

"Train tickets? How'd you manage to get these?" Vera asked.

"Used to work on the rails," Havert explained. "My daughter and I…had a falling out a while back. She wanted more than what this farm and I could provide, and I was too stubborn to listen. I thought I would take the train to visit her and apologize—but I never worked up the nerve. And now I'm far too old to be riding the tracks."

"We couldn't possibly take these," Emaline began.

"Please. If you don't, they'll just go to waste." Havert sighed. "I only ask you one favor in return."

"Yes?" Emaline inquired.

"If you happen to come across my daughter while on your journey, would you tell her that I'm sorry?"

Emaline took Havert's hands into her own. "Of course," she promised.

Chapter Five

After a quick breakfast, Vera and Emaline left Havert's farm. They walked through the desert, the temperature rising along with the morning sun. A few miles from the canyon was a train station raised up onto a metal platform. An iron train with clockwork wheels sat on the tracks, hissing out jets of steam. At the sight of it, Emaline's eyes widened with awe.

"I've never seen such an amazing machine," she said, gawking. "Do you think it will take us all the way to Jungo?"

"Unfortunately, no," Vera answered. "This train only runs between two of the major cities, and this is its midway point."

"I see," Emaline sighed.

"But on the bright side, it will save us a few days' worth of travel. And then once we're in the city, we can resupply," Vera said reassuringly.

They walked up onto the platform, passing metal benches and looming lampposts. People stood in a line outside of the train door, handing their tickets to the conductor before being let inside.

As they waited in line, a young woman passed by Emaline, exiting the train. There was something familiar about her curly blonde hair and sky-blue eyes. The young woman leaned against the railing of the platform, staring off into the distance.

"Perhaps I shouldn't have come," the young woman mumbled
to herself.

"Excuse me," Emaline said, tapping her on the shoulder.

The young woman turned her big, blue eyes to Emaline.
"Yes?"

"You wouldn't happen to have a relative living out there,
would you?" Emaline asked.

"Yes, my father," she answered. "Have you seen him?"

"Yes, and he left us with a message for you. He wanted to say
that he was sorry."

The young woman's eyes brimmed with tears, which she
hurriedly wiped away. "Thank you," she said quietly, stepping
off the platform and trekking out toward the horizon.

"Do you think they'll make up?" Emaline asked Vera.

"There's rarely a tear that can't be mended, not if all the
pieces are still there," Vera answered.

"Do you think the world is the same?"

"I don't understand what you mean."

"The world broke, but that doesn't mean that it can't be put
back together, does it?" Emaline asked. "There used to be
billions of us, but now we're a dwindling few—post the dramatic
climax and now just the last few words at the end of the book:
Earth turned to Epilogue," she said. "But an ending is never

really the end, is it? The purpose of an epilogue is to plant seeds of thought, to give life to the next idea."

"That's pretty philosophical," Vera teased.

"Well, do you?"

"Do I what?"

"Do you think we can fix the world?" Emaline asked, a desperation in her gaze.

Vera stared at her with unsure eyes, her lips moving without sound.

"Next!" the conductor barked.

They had been so enthralled in conversation that they hadn't realized they were at the front of the line. Vera handed the conductor the two tickets, which he hurriedly stamped and slid into his pocket.

"Next!" he called, moving aside.

Vera and Emaline stepped onto the train and slipped into an unoccupied seat. Rows of leather booths ran down the length of the train car, lit by small square windows. Luggage was crammed into narrow shelves hanging from the ceiling by thin metal chains.

"I'm surprised you never rode the train before," Vera said. "Lots of cityfolk use it to avoid walking in the desert."

"My family tended to keep to themselves. My mother was especially… protective," Emaline explained. "I was rarely allowed to leave the house, let alone the city."

The train heaved forward, gliding down the track. Emaline watched out the window as the scenery passed her by, snacking quictly on one of the pastries she had hidden in her satchel. Just then, she spotted a cloud of sand rippling across the desert. Squinting, Emaline could make out a hoverbike with fan wheels propelled forward by the wind. The front of the bike looked like the face of a cackling jackal, made of scrap metal with the headlights for its eyes. Emaline watched as a second bike rode up, then a third, until an entire parade of them were following alongside the train.

"I think we may have a problem," Emaline began, turning toward Vera's seat only to find it empty.

Vera was standing, her pistol drawn toward the door at the front of the train. The other passengers all stared at her, murmuring worriedly to one another.

With a loud hiss, the train door slid open, and Wylie stepped through with a snaggletooth smile. "You know, a jackal's only as good as his pack," he said, gesturing to the window.

"I'm more of the lone wolf type, myself," Vera said coolly, cocking her pistol.

Wylie's eyes flickered to Emaline and glimmered mischievously. "Not anymore."

Before Vera could reach her, Emaline was yanked out of her seat by a burly man in a leather jacket. Emaline squirmed and kicked, but the man seemed unfazed by her attacks.

"What do you want?" Vera asked, turning back toward Wylie.

"I have a reputation to uphold as the leader of the Golden Jackal Gang," Wylie explained, talking with his hands. "Having two little ladies disrespect me in my own territory isn't something I can let slide."

Wylie walked past the rows of trembling passengers until he was face to face with Vera, their noses nearly touching.

"My problem isn't with you; it's with Miss Prissy, over there," he said, nodding to Emaline. "I'll make you a deal. Hand over the girl, and these people get to leave this train alive."

Vera considered the idea a moment, then nodded. "Take her. She was slowing me down anyway," she said, shrugging.

"What?" Emaline muttered.

"You heard her," Wylie said, looking at his lackey.

The burly man swung Emaline over his shoulder and carried her toward the door.

"What about Jungo? What about our deal?" Emaline cried, pounding on the thug's back.

"I've always believed that a deal isn't proper until you've shaken on it," Vera said, holding her hand out toward Wylie.

"Couldn't have said it better myself," Wylie chuckled.

The second his hand wrapped around hers, Vera crushed it. She yanked him forward, sending his stomach hurtling into her raised knee. Wylie let out a pained wheeze as his lungs compressed, gasping for air. Before he could recover, Vera hooked her arm around Wylie's neck and held the pistol against the side of his head.

"Call off your gang," she warned.

"You could have killed me back in town…but you didn't." Wylie panted, licking his lips. "You don't have what it takes."

Vera hovered her finger over the trigger. "Want to find out?"

"F-fine!" Wylie snarled. "Let her go," he ordered his lackey.

"But, boss—" the thug began.

"Did you not hear me? I said let her go!" Wylie growled louder.

The thug heaved Emaline off of his shoulder and gently placed her back onto the ground. Emaline dusted off her dress, turned, and then kicked him in the groin as hard as she could. The thug collapsed onto his knees, his arms buried between his legs.

Vera released Wylie from her grasp and shoved him forward.

"You're all bark and no bite," Wylie spat. He slipped out the door and leaped down through the gap in the train cars, landing on the back of a hoverbike, his lackey following closely behind.

"I'm sorry," Emaline said to Vera. "I thought you'd really handed me over to those brutes."

"I've done a lot of bad things in my life, but I've never gone back on a promise," Vera said.

The train lurched forward, quickly gaining speed.

Vera stumbled into Emaline, who caught her fall.

"That's not supposed to be happening, is it?" Emaline asked anxiously.

"No, it's not," Vera said, thrusting open the slider door between the cars. Tentatively, she stepped onto the kissing hooks that locked the cars together and climbed into the locomotive. Inside was a wide, curved window with an intricate control panel beneath. The conductor was slumped against the back wall, unconscious. At the head of the control panel was a scrawny figure in a fox-eared hoodie. They yanked off a lever from the panel and tossed it aside with an annoyed grumble.

At the sound of Vera's footsteps against the metal floor, they perked up and whipped back around. They glared at her, a bandana obscuring the bottom of their face. "Don't mess with the Jackals," they hissed, slamming their fist onto a red button on the wall.

The emergency door at the side of the locomotive flew open, letting in a flood of rippling wind. The stranger leaped out the door and landed on Wylie's hoverbike, riding off with the rest of the gang. As they veered off toward the horizon, Vera could hear the cackle of their laughter.

"What's happening?" Emaline asked, pulling herself into the locomotive.

"They overrode the speed limiters and ripped out the brakes," Vera explained.

"We can't stop the train?" Emaline said. "Well, how far are we from the city?"

"At this speed, I'd say about five minutes."

"We'll crash," Emaline murmured fearfully.

"Can't jump out either. At this speed, we'd hit the sand dead." Vera peered warily out of the emergency exit.

Emaline knelt beside the unconscious conductor and shook him by the shoulders. "Come on, wake up," she urged, slapping him gently back and forth.

"Wha—?" the conductor moaned groggily, holding his aching head.

"The train's out of control. The brake lever is broken, and we're heading straight for the city," Emaline explained. "You have to tell us how to stop the train."

The conductor coughed weakly. "There's an emergency brake, but it's on the roof."

"The roof? How are we supposed to reach it up there?" Emaline asked.

"Well, usually there's a long hook we use to pull it from the inside, but your friend severed the chain," the conductor explained.

"We'll have to do it manually," Vera murmured. She spotted the ladder at the side of the locomotive and began to climb up it.

"Where are you going?" Emaline hissed.

"To the roof," Vera said, popping open the hatch at the top of the ladder.

A trail of handles lined the roof, allowing Vera to pull herself along the length of the train, fighting against the wind. A few feet ahead, in the back of the locomotive's roof was a divot with a bright red lever.

"Ow," a small whimper echoed from behind.

Vera peered back over her shoulder and spotted Emaline climbing along the ladder behind her. Her delicate hands had turned red and blistered from touching the searing metal.

"What are you doing? Go back inside!" Vera barked.

"I've spent my entire life inside!" Emaline barked back. "I'm sick of people acting like I'm helpless—like I'm something to be protected."

"You're not helpless," Vera said, softer than before. "But as my client, I can't let you get hurt."

"You're the one who's always running head-first into danger! I know you prefer to be alone—I know you had to be in order to survive—but you're not alone anymore. So please, just let me help."

"*You* hired *me*. That means I'm responsible for you, not the other way around. As my client, you shouldn't have to—"

"Would you stop calling me that!" Emaline yelled. "Not when I thought we were friends…"

For the first time, Vera really looked into Emaline's eyes. They were like two pools of rich, green water with speckles of tangerine.

Vera wrinkled her lip and furrowed her brow, thinking. "Fine," she sighed. "You're your own woman. You can make your own decisions."

Emaline grasped the next railing, embracing the burn as it met her fingers. Tentatively, they made their way toward the brake, trying not to lose their grip. Vera reached out and grasped the red lever, yanking it back. The train screeched, its metal wheels sparking against the track as it began to slow.

The sudden jolt knocked Vera's hand loose from the railing, sending her flying forward. Her vision spun: blue sky, yellow sand, gray metal. Her body hurtled through the air, skipping down the train like a stone on a lake. Just as she was about to be thrown off the side of the train, something grabbed hold of her wrist. She peered up and saw Emaline holding on to her with one hand while grasping the railing with the other.

"What would you do without me?" Emaline teased, sweat rolling down her cheek.

The train cruised into the station, coming to a steady halt right before the end of the tracks. Steam bellowed out of the train's chimney with a piercing whistle, announcing its arrival. As the passengers flooded out from the train doors, they stopped and peered up at the two women dangling off the side.

"Could someone fetch a ladder?" Emaline called down.

Chapter Six

"You think they'd be a little more grateful for saving their lives," Vera sighed, staring dismally at the handful of oreales in her hand.

"Well, it sort of was our fault the passengers were in danger in the first place," Emaline said.

They walked together down the hot pavement, past towering buildings of metal, frozen in mid-decay. It was a makeshift city built off of the bones of whatever the Old Ones had left behind. Signs hung over the street and jutted off the sides of the buildings, each written in a different language than the last. Water pumps with coin slots built into the top were stationed every few feet.

Emaline turned her attention across the street, where frail figures were sitting on the curb and sleeping in the shadowed alleyways. Between the rows of tall buildings was a wide pathway filled with people carrying whatever goods they'd acquired for the day; others led oxen-driven carts or wove between the crowd on mopeds. The entire city seemed to move like one shaky, humid breath.

"Welcome to Sundial City, the second-largest establishment in all of Epilogue," Vera said. "Is this anything like the city you're from?"

"No, not really. I'm from the Golden Valley," Emaline said. "It's a lot smaller than this."

"Jungo's pretty far from the Valley." Vera whistled as they walked. "Do you know why your dad wanted his ashes spread there, of all places?"

"I've never been there to see it myself, but my father always said it was the most beautiful place in the world," Emaline explained. "He visited it often, sometimes for months at a time. I always wanted to come along, but my mother forbade me."

"I never answered your question back at the station. About whether I think we can fix the world or not," Vera said abruptly, catching Emaline by surprise. "You're one of those glass-half-full kind of girls, right? Well, I don't have as much faith in people, let's put it that way."

"It's not like because I'm an optimist, it means that I think everyone's a good person," Emaline said, staring down at the cement. "But I think we don't give ourselves enough credit. Being alive is hard. But despite the hardships, we're still kind. Well, not all of us, but most."

"I don't know if kindness can save us," Vera sighed. "Maybe that's why we're going extinct: that damned human morality. Or maybe it's because we never listened to it enough." She chuckled to herself.

"I guess I just don't see the point in it," Emaline said quietly.

"The point of what?"

"Thinking that we're only capable of bad things."

Vera sighed. "I'm just being realistic."

"So am I," Emaline said. "Even though I've only been in the desert a few days, I've already met a lot of kind people."

"You also met Wylie."

"We're all just doing what we can to survive. I'm not saying that that makes his actions right or even good, but they make sense, at least," Emaline said. "Speaking of, do you think we'll have a run-in with him while we're here?"

"It's unlikely. The Jackals tend to stay on the east side of the desert, and they rarely come into the cities," Vera said. "Besides, all Wylie wanted to do was make himself look good. As far as his gang knows, we're dead, and they won; I doubt Wylie's going to come to check on us and ruin that."

They stumbled upon a gap in the buildings, a wide alleyway filled with wooden stalls. Each stall was unique, selling a different assortment of wares. Lights were strung between the buildings, lighting the market as the sky darkened with dusk.

"Can we go there?" Emaline asked excitedly, pointing to the market.

"My job is to get you to Jungo, not to take you shopping," Vera said, crossing her arms.

Emaline shrugged and scooped half of the oreales from Vera's hand.

"What do you think you're doing?" Vera asked.

"Taking my cut," Emaline said, walking toward the market.

"What cut? *You're* paying *me*," Vera spat, trailing after her.

"Those people gave us this money because we stopped the train. Since it was a joint effort, I think I deserve at least fifty percent of the profit."

"*Fifty percent*? I was the one who pulled the lever!" Vera snapped.

"And if it weren't for me, you'd be roadkill." Emaline strolled up to a stall decorated with jewelry made of recycled items: bottle cap bracelets and jar lid necklaces. "What do you think?" she asked, holding a pair of pen cap earrings against the side of her head.

Vera scowled at her but then sighed, letting her features soften. She stood next to Emaline and grabbed a pair of sea glass earrings. "These would be better. They match your eyes."

Emaline's dark skin flushed a rosy red. Hurriedly, she hid her gawking eyes and shyly combed back her hair. "You think so? Well, I guess I might as well get a souvenir. Who knows if I'll ever be able to come back here again," she said, handing the vendor her oreales.

"Could you…?" Emaline held the earrings out toward Vera. "I don't have a mirror."

Vera took the pair of green sea glass earrings and carefully hooked them through each of Emaline's ears. "There," Vera said.

The earrings jingled and danced as Emaline spun on the heel of her shoe, sending her skirt flaring out like a blooming flower. "Well? Worth the purchase?"

Vera felt warmth grow across her cheeks and over the bridge of her nose. She wiped the blush from her face and cleared her throat. "They look nice," she said.

Emaline smiled, and Vera was helpless from blushing an even darker shade of red.

"Come on. We might as well get some supplies while we're here," Vera said, marching ahead.

Side by side, they wandered through the market, taking in the sights and sounds. The rectangle of sky visible between the buildings was filled with a starry nothingness. A cacophony of chatter resonated from the alley, full of people trying to get the best bargain.

Vera stopped in front of a stall run by a girl with straight black hair tied back by a red ribbon. She had on a loose tank top with a smiling cat on the front and a pair of ripped jean shorts. Packaged rations were stacked in neat piles across the counter, separated by flavor.

"How much can I get for this?" Vera asked, holding out the fistful of oreales.

The girl leaned off her stool and counted the money under her breath. Silently, she grabbed a random assortment of rations and slid them into Vera's open hand.

"Thank you kindly," Vera said, tipping her hat.

Just then, a man walked up beside her, adorned in a silver robe. He had short, pale hair and a boyish face. A jagged scar was carved through his left eye. At the sight of him, Vera stiffened.

Slowly, she stuffed the rations into her satchel and motioned for Emaline to back away. "We need to go. Now."

"Why?" Emaline whispered back.

"Because that man is with Aquis," Vera hissed. "You can always tell by the scar."

"Sister, have the clouds been kind?" the man asked the vendor.

"My name is Kasumi. And I am *not* your sister," the girl spat.

"All of us are brothers and sisters under Aquis," the man chuckled. "But you've been slipping lately, haven't you, sister?"

"On payments?" Kasumi laughed, slamming her hands against the counter. "And how exactly do you expect us to be able to pay? This is the Light Market. We don't come here because we want to. We come here out of necessity, selling what we can so we don't shrivel up in the streets. And you come here and tell us to pay your fees for the very water *we* unearthed?" she snarled.

"No one can own water," the man said. "It is as free as the tides themselves."

"Oh? You and your little friends don't have any jurisdiction over who gets water and who doesn't?" Kasumi asked, crossing her arms.

"We do not own the water. We're simply vessels for Altera's blessing, helping determine who is deserving of it and who is not," the man explained.

"You take what little we have in order to give us what we already deserve," Kasumi spat. "No one *deserves* to die of thirst. *That*, you should be able to understand…unless becoming a vessel has cost you your heart?"

"I see." The man sighed disappointedly. "Well, if you would not rather die of thirst…" he said, whipping out a dagger from his baggy sleeves.

Kasumi simply glared at him, unafraid.

Before his dagger could reach her, Emaline moved, grabbing it with her bare hand. She grasped the silver blade in her palm, blood dripping from her fingers.

"You are unfamiliar to me, sister," the man said, speaking politely even as his blade dug into Emaline's skin. "Could you tell me your name?"

"Emaline Gales," she spat, keeping a firm grasp around the dagger.

"Mine is Yol," the man said. "Sister, I believe you are mistaken. This woman has betrayed Altera's gift by denying it her fortune."

"And could you tell me what a water deity would want with human currency?" Emaline asked.

"It is a symbol of your loyalty, of your devotion," Yol began.

"The only reason these people are loyal to you is because they're afraid—because they'll die if they aren't," Emaline spat.

"Ah, I see." The man sighed, dropping his head to his chest. "You are a dissident as well." The man pulled back his dagger from her clenched hand and raised it up into the air above her chest.

Vera pulled her pistol out from its holster and pressed it against the man's cheek in one swift motion. "I wouldn't do that if I were you, *partner*."

The standoff began to gather the attention of passersby, drawing in the other vendors. Soon enough, they were surrounded by a hollering mob.

"We're sick of paying your fees!"

"Give us back our water!"

"Down with Aquis!"

Yol, quickly realizing he was outnumbered, slowly withdrew his dagger and hid it back into his sleeve. He glared with loathing at Emaline and whispered, "Your actions will not go unpunished." He turned and trudged out of the alley as the crowd broke into a fit of cheers.

A vendor selling butte beer uncorked one of the barrels at his side and filled a pint, thrusting it into the air. "Free drinks to celebrate!" he roared. Other vendors followed suit, yelling out discounted prices for their wares. A young woman traveling with a violin began to play an upbeat melody, filling the market with music. Amongst the mass of drinking and dancing was Emaline, cradling her bleeding hand with Vera glaring down at her.

"What were you thinking?" Vera grumbled, taking a square of cloth from a textile stall and wrapping it around Emaline's hand.

"What was I supposed to do?" Emaline asked.

"This is *exactly* what I warned you about! What did you do? Talk. And what did it lead to? Trouble," Vera said, tying the cloth into a knot. "You managed to piss off the Jackals, and now we have Aquis on our trail!"

"Is this a bad time?" Kasumi interrupted, walking up to them.

"No, it's—you're fine," Emaline said, glancing anxiously at Vera.

"I just wanted to say thank you," Kasumi said. "You're travelers, aren't you? Do you have a place to stay for the night?"

"You know what? We don't," Vera said.

"Then I may be able to repay the favor," Kasumi replied with a half grin.

Chapter Seven

Kasumi led Emaline and Vera out of the Light Market and into the darkness of the city. They traveled down the quiet streets to a tall brick building with long, rectangular windows. Kasumi walked to the side of the building and began climbing up the rusted fire escape.

Vera cocked an eyebrow. "What's wrong? Is the front door broken?"

"No, but the elevator is, and the stairs are steep," Kasumi said. "Trust me; this is the quickest way to the top."

Emaline and Vera climbed up the flight of twisted stairs to a window lit with golden light. Kasumi pushed open the window and slid inside, motioning for them to follow suit. It was a modest space, cluttered but clean. Framed family photos hung on the walls wherever there was space. They'd climbed into a kitchen which was filled with the heavenly aroma of citrus and ginger.

"Sobo, we have guests," Kasumi called.

An old woman with a happy, wrinkled face was hunched over the stovetop, obscured by steam. "Oh, it's been a long time since we had those," she chuckled, wiping her fogged glasses with the corner of her sweater.

"I owe these two my life. They interfered when an Aquis official came to the market," Kasumi explained.

"Then I'll have to make them quite the delicacy." The old woman patted Emaline's rosy cheeks.

"We appreciate you letting us stay here," Emaline said politely.

"It's no trouble. I've missed making food for four," the old woman said.

"My parents used to live here, but then Aquis…" Kasumi tried to explain. "Anyway, I run the stall now."

"And she does a damn good job," the old woman said, stirring a boiling pot with a wooden spoon.

"*Sobo*," Kasumi scolded, putting her hands on her hips.

"What?" the old woman teased.

"Grandmothers shouldn't swear," Kasumi chuckled.

"Yeah? Well, this one does."

"Um, ma'am—" Emaline began.

"You can call me Hana," the old woman interrupted.

"Well then, Hana, I actually made most of our meals back home if you wanted a helping hand in the kitchen?" Emaline offered.

"I could always use a good sous chef. Kasumi's a terrible cook," Hana whispered behind her hand, cringing.

Kasumi rolled her eyes but smiled.

Emaline tossed on an apron and began to chop a daikon radish into thin circular disks.

"I didn't know you could cook," Vera said quietly, peering over Emaline's shoulder.

"There's a lot you don't know about me," Emaline teased under her breath.

While Emaline and Hana worked side by side in the kitchen, Vera set the table. A loud humming echoed from the living room as Kasumi blew up the air mattress.

"Dinner's ready!" Hana announced, bringing a ceramic dish out of the oven.

Soon enough, the kitchen table was filled with plates of delicious dishes: tonkatsu pork and daikon radish salad with a sesame dressing.

"This might be your best meal yet, Sobo," Kasumi said, her face lighting up at the first bite.

"Thank your friend. She really knows her cooking," Hana laughed.

Emaline couldn't help blushing at the compliment. It had been a while since she had been in a kitchen, and she had forgotten the pride of making a meal by hand. For the past week, all she'd eaten were cold beans and nutrition bars, so her mouth was thankful for the different flavors and textures.

"Of course, this could never compare to Old World cuisine," Hana sighed. "But we make do with what we have."

"This doesn't taste like just 'making do,'" Emaline chuckled. "You're quite the chef."

"Flattery won't get you far in the desert, but it'll work just fine on me." Hana laughed, loading Emaline's plate with an extra helping of tonkatsu.

After their plates had been washed and the night had grown long, Hana and Kasumi retired to their bedrooms to sleep. Vera laid on the pull-out couch, gazing at the ceiling with scowling eyes. Emaline watched her from the mattress on the floor, tucked beneath a quilted blanket.

"What's wrong?" Emaline asked.

"I don't like not being able to see the stars," Vera murmured.

"You know, it's kinda funny seeing you like this."

"Like what?" Vera asked, turning onto her side.

"I've just never seen a cowboy on a pull-out couch before," Emaline chuckled softly, trying to keep her voice low.

They both broke into a fit of hushed laughter.

"I'm sorry," Emaline said as their laughter quieted. "You were right. I always get us into trouble."

"That's not true. The only reason we have a roof over our heads right now is because of you," Vera said. "This is Epilogue.

Trouble follows you the second you walk out the door. That's just the way things are."

"Do you still prefer to be a 'lone wolf'?" Emaline taunted gently.

"Always did, but now I'm not so sure. I guess it takes company to realize how quiet the night really is."

The thunder of passersby rumbled from the streets below, alongside the rattle of wooden carts. The chatter from the Light Market carried on the air, accompanied by the nonsensical singing of drunks at the bar across the street. The night was filled with noise, but to Vera, it all sounded like silence.

"Once our deal is done…do you think we can—?" Vera began to ask.

When she received no answer, she peered down and found Emaline fast asleep, snoring softly. "Good night, Princess," she whispered into the darkness of the living room.

. . .

Vera rarely let herself fall into a deep sleep, but something about that night, whether it was the food or the company, convinced her to make an exception. Unfortunately, her sleep was cut short. In the midst of a pleasant dream, Vera was shaken awake.

51

She blinked open her eyes and was surprised to see Kasumi hovering above her. "What's wrong?" Vera groaned, sitting up.

"Aquis officials. I saw them enter from downstairs," Kasumi explained.

"Question is, are they here for you or for us?" Vera asked, standing.

"Probably just killing two birds with one stone," Kasumi muttered.

Vera peered down at Emaline's sleeping figure on the floor, watching the rise and fall of her breathing beneath the blanket. She knelt beside her and gently shook her shoulder.

"What is it?" Emaline yawned, rubbing the sleep from her eyes.

"We have to leave. They've found us."

The three women packed in the dark, grabbing whatever essentials they could carry.

Hana pushed open her bedroom door, shuffling down the hall in a pair of fuzzy slippers and a bathrobe. "Leaving already? I haven't even made breakfast."

"Sobo, there's no time. They know we're here," Kasumi explained.

Hana's plump pink lips thinned until they became two fine lines. Her wrinkled, sun-spotted hands shook at her side, balled into fists. "Those Aquis dogs," she cursed. "They took my son—the one I raised in this very apartment. Then they took the love of his life, your mother. And now they're here to finish us off? Well, when they come, they're going to get more than what they bargained for!"

Kasumi walked over to her grandmother and hugged her. "You're all I have left. I can't lose you too," she said quietly. "This isn't a fight worth having. Not here, not now."

"Then let's go," Hana said, petting Kasumi's soft, black hair. She disappeared into her bedroom, reemerging moments later dressed and carrying a packed bag across her back.

"It's taken them a long time to get up here," Emaline muttered anxiously.

"I told you: steep stairs," Kasumi chuckled.

Just then, a heavy knock pounded against the door. When no one answered, a thudding began, buckling the door at its hinges.

"Time to go," Vera said, flinging open the kitchen window.

Together, the four of them raced down the fire escape into the alley.

"I'm sorry. If I hadn't interfered with that Aquis official—" Emaline began.

Kasumi put a hand on her shoulder and smiled. "I'd be dead right now," she finished. "Aquis was our enemy long before you came around. We knew this would happen eventually."

"Where will you go?" Emaline asked.

"Don't worry about us." Kasumi gestured to her tank top. "A cat always lands on its feet."

Chapter Eight

The city's neon signs and bright windows faded as the dawn began to break. Emaline and Vera parted ways with Kasumi and her grandmother, sneaking through the back alleys of the city. As they were wandering, they came across a set of stone steps leading down to a shallow canal. Up ahead, along the canal, was a group of children hollering at passersby.

One of them, a scrawny boy in a flat cap, walked in front of Emaline's path, holding out a tin can. "Spare some oreales?" the boy asked.

"What do you need them for?" Emaline asked curiously.

"For what else? We need 'em for the pay pumps."

"Pay pumps?"

"Yeah, for each oreale you put in, you get one pump of water," the boy explained.

Emaline glared at the row of metal pipes jutting up from the concrete. In the Golden Valley, where the wealthy isolated themselves from the rest of the world, there were no wells or pay pumps, just faucets ripe with water. Emaline's eyes moved down to the canal, watching the dark-green water glide along the grimy basin.

"I wouldn't drink that if I were you," the boy warned, catching Emaline's glance. "My friend got so thirsty once that he drank from the canal, and he's been deathly ill ever since."

"Tell you what; I'll give you some oreales, but I want to give you something else as well," Emaline said.

"Have you forgotten that Aquis is hunting us down?" Vera hissed under her breath. "We don't have time for—"

"There's always time for kindness," Emaline said, dropping the last of her oreales into the tin can. She dug around in her skirt pocket and pulled out a disk-shaped device, offering it to the boy.

"What is it?" the boy asked curiously, taking the device into his hands.

"A water purifier that I designed," Emaline explained. "It can even turn dirty water like that into something safe and drinkable. That way, you'll never have to use a pay pump again. Sorry, it's so small; they don't seem to work if I make them any bigger—well, not yet."

"No, this is…very nice, thank you," the boy said, gawking at the amazing device.

Just then, footsteps thundered from behind, echoing down the stone steps.

Vera grabbed Emaline's arm and dragged her behind a stack of fishing barrels. Vera watched in the crack between the barrels as four Aquis officials raced down the canal, stopping in front of the boy. They each had a scar cutting through their left eye and wore robes with a two-tailed koi fish embroidered on the back.

"Have you seen two women matching these descriptions?" one asked, holding up a wanted poster.

The boy shrugged nonchalantly, pocketing the water purifier. "Never seen them in my life."

"Well, if you do, you know who to tell," the official said gruffly, retreating back up the stone steps.

"They're gone," the boy called, turning toward the barrels.

"Thanks for the save," Vera said, tipping her hat.

"Thank your friend," the boy called back, tipping his own.

Emaline gave the boy a kind smile as she walked down the rest of the canal and up the stairs to the streets above. Together, she and Vera trekked through the maze of buildings and bridges of Sundial City until they reached a long concrete tunnel.

"This should take us back out into the desert," Vera explained.

The inside of the tunnel was lit by fluorescent bulbs, illuminating generations of graffiti. Spiders watched warily from the corners, hidden in their silk cradles. Emaline walked close to Vera, anxiously peering back over her shoulder to make sure they hadn't been followed.

"I kinda feel like…humanity's going through a tunnel right now," Vera said.

"Oh?" Emaline hummed.

"We're all just walking down this endless tunnel, unsure what we'll find at the end," Vera explained. "Maybe it'll be the light of salvation, or maybe we'll just fade further into darkness. My bet's on the latter."

"You always talk as if humanity's already gone," Emaline teased.

"Feels that way sometimes," Vera sighed with a smile.

Emaline playfully nudged Vera in the side. "But *we're* still here."

"Yeah, we're still here," Vera chuckled softly.

A faint light began to glimmer at the end of the tunnel. Vera peeked out into the blinding sunlight, shielding her eyes with her hand. Even though the heat was dizzyingly intense, as the rays caressed her face, it felt like the touch of an old friend.

• • •

Emaline and Vera walked along the dunes, past cacti and acacia trees, until the sun had nearly completed its trek across the sky. A tilted billboard jutted out from the side of a high dune, looming over them. The signage had wasted away long ago, leaving only the dark metal banner behind.

"That thing's a relic," Vera said.

"What is it?" Emaline asked.

"A billboard. They used to line roads and highways."

"What for?"

"To advertise stuff," Vera said. "You know, like makeup and insurance—stuff we have no use for in Epilogue."

They sat side by side beneath the billboard, lounging in its shadow. Emaline soaked up the shade, enjoying a break from the sun. Vera tossed her a ration bar labeled, "red pepper potato," from her satchel.

Emaline grimaced. "These things never taste like what they're supposed to be."

"Whatever's on the label is just a seasoning they add on top. The rest is all pure nutrients—everything you need to keep going." Vera took an eager bite of her own ration bar, chewing thoughtfully.

"Do you ever wish you'd been born in the Old World?" Emaline asked, peering up at the billboard, trying to imagine what it may have looked like in its prime.

"Sometimes," Vera answered. "But life wasn't easy back then either."

"I suppose so," Emaline said. "What do you miss the most about it?"

"…Butterflies."

Emaline chortled.

"What?" Vera asked, red with embarrassment.

"It's nothing—your answer just caught me off guard, is all. You have to admit, it's sort of humorous that a gunslinger would miss butterflies, of all things."

"I'm not *just* a gunslinger…" Vera mumbled, pouting. "Besides, it's the apocalypse; everyone has a weapon on them."

"Then what are you when you're not—" Emaline took off Vera's cowboy hat and held it out in front of her "—*this*?"

"I play guitar," Vera said awkwardly, not used to talking about herself. "And I whittle whenever I have the time. Or sometimes I—" She cut herself off.

"Sometimes you what?"

"I may *dabble* in poetry," Vera said, blushing.

Emaline's eyes flung open, and her mouth hung ajar. "I used to read loads of poetry back home," she said excitedly. "You have to recite me some of your work sometime."

"It's nothing spectacular," Vera said, waving away the idea. "Besides, what's the use of a poet in a world like this? Give it fifty years, and my words will be lost."

"Maybe they will, but maybe they won't," Emaline said. "Even if we're gone, what we choose to leave behind will remain. I can only read poetry because people chose to salvage books, even as the world was crumbling down around them. They thought the words they held meant something—could mean something for future generations."

"I doubt what I have to say will be remembered with such admiration," Vera chuckled.

"Maybe not. But you enjoy it, don't you?" Emaline said, more as a statement than a question. "Then you should continue to do it. And maybe it won't be admired by millions, but someone may look at it someday and *feel* something, and isn't that enough?"

Vera stared at Emaline, perplexed. "You always manage to amaze me."

"Amaze? Really?" Emaline said, flustered.

"It's the way you talk about things, about the world," Vera explained. "I don't know if I'll ever be able to believe that it's true…but you make me want to."

"Believe what?"

"That the world's still beautiful."

The two women looked into each other's eyes as if to find some hidden message written behind the other's gaze. Their faces leaned toward one another's, their noses nearly touching.

Vera frowned and pulled away, gently taking her cowboy hat from Emaline's hands and placing it back onto her head. "We should start making camp. Sun's going down," she said.

. . .

Typically, it was a noise or a smell that woke Emaline, but this time, it was a feeling. Groggily, she rose up onto her elbows off her cot. Earlier, she and Vera had pitched a small tent that they'd purchased at the Light Market. It was nothing more than a tarp with some metal rods, but it kept the sand out, and that's all that really mattered.

Emaline spotted Vera sitting at the front of the tent, peeking out of the flap. She could tell it was still nighttime from the darkness looming outside and the cold on her skin.

"What is it?" Emaline mumbled, still half asleep.

Vera held a finger to her lips, motioning to be quiet, then pointed through the gap in the tent flap. Emaline sat beside her and peered up into the starlit sky. Gigantic, albino bats were flying overhead, their eyes glistening red in the moonlight. Emaline studied the bats from afar, the angle of their webbed, veiny wings, the way their pointed noses perfectly resembled a capital V.

"Are they dangerous?" Emaline asked.

"Only to bugs," Vera said.

"…Do you think we're changing?"

"How so?"

"These bats, those coyotes from the farm—the animals are all changing. They're much bigger than they used to be, and a whole lot more deadly," Emaline explained. "So I wonder if we're becoming something new—something different from what we were before."

"Something better, I hope," Vera said quietly.

"So why butterflies?"

"You're still on about that?" Vera chuckled. "I guess it's because they make me feel hopeful."

Emaline nodded, urging her to go on.

"If something as delicate and gentle as a butterfly can exist, then things can't be *that* bad, can they?" Vera explained. "Of course, I've only ever seen them in picture books."

"Maybe we lost it—the type of hope that allows little, helpless things to survive," Emaline muttered. "But maybe someday, it'll come back to us."

She was so enamored by the strange creatures in the sky that she hadn't even realized she was shivering.

"Here," Vera said, holding out part of the woven blanket that was draped over her shoulders. Emaline, a little hesitantly, scooted closer and wrapped herself in the blanket, grateful for its warmth. The two women gazed at the sea of stars above them, dreaming of the world before their own.

Chapter Nine

The next morning, at the break of dawn, Emaline made a small fire. She couldn't help smiling with a twinge of pride as the kindling caught flame. She grabbed the black metal saucepan from Vera's satchel and a bag of grits, simmering them over the fire. She scooped the tan mush out of the pot and into her mouth, frowning.

"Flavorless," she grumbled. She looked side to side and spotted a round, spiked cactus with pink flowers. "Vera told me those were edible, didn't she?"

She walked over to the cactus and inspected it, plucking a handful of its small, candy-shaped flowers. When she returned to the fire, she tossed the flowers into the pot and stirred. With a nervous crinkle in her lips, she took another bite, blushing at its taste.

Vera popped her head out of the tent flap, sniffing hungrily at the air. "What smells good?" She yawned, walking toward the fire.

"I made you breakfast," Emaline said, offering her a bowl.

Vera took the bowl into her hands and took a hesitant bite. Her eyes flung open with surprise at the rich, sweet flavor that hit her tongue. "How did you manage to make grits taste this good?" she asked.

With a silent, confident smile, Emaline pointed to the plump
cactus standing a few feet away.

"You're getting better at identifying plants, and that fire you
made is just about perfect."

"Really?" Emaline asked, starry-eyed.

"You know, I think desert life might suit you."

Vera's half-grin and lidded eyes made Emaline's ears burn
red. But her daze was broken as a cry rang through the still
morning air. Someone, somewhere in the distance, was yelling
for help.

Without hesitation, Emaline darted across the sand toward the
noise, Vera following close behind. They hiked up a short dune
and looked down over the valley below. There was a person
half-buried in a pool of wet, thick sand. Their arms flailed
wildly, trying to claw their way back to solid ground. Their face
was obscured beneath a scarf that wrapped over their mouth and
over their head to block out the sun. A pair of orange-tinted
goggles was strapped over their eyes.

"Quicksand?" Emaline muttered under her breath.

Vera scoffed. "Well, that idiot got themself into that mess.
They can get themselves out. Let's get back to our breakfast."

"We can't just leave them," Emaline said.

"If you're going to make us stop and help every sad sap we
find, it's going to take a lot longer to get to Jungo."

"I don't care how long it takes. I'll get to Jungo *and* help whoever needs it."

"You don't even know them! They could be a criminal."

"You didn't know who I was when you decided to help me."

"Maybe so, but I knew you had a big wallet." Vera smirked.

Emaline narrowed her eyes and scowled at her. She reached into her bag and pulled out a bundle of rope.

"What are you doing?" Vera asked.

"Going after them. You don't have to help." Emaline began to tie the rope around her waist.

"Why are you always so eager to help people?" Vera asked, softer than before.

"There have been moments in my life where I wish someone would have helped me, but they didn't. Sometimes you can't save yourself. Sometimes you need someone to give you a hand," Emaline explained. "Besides, in my experience, if you help someone, then they're more likely to help you back. And in a world like this, it seems like we could use all the help we could get."

Vera sighed and untied the rope around Emaline's waist, cinching it around her own. She shoved the end of the rope into Emaline's hands. "Don't let go, okay?" she said firmly.

Emaline blushed and nodded, taken aback.

Vera waddled into the cement-like substance, each step growing heavier than the last. "Grab my hand!" she barked.

The stranger leaned forward and stretched out their hand as far as it would go, straining the fingers. Their body continued to slowly sink deeper, the sand rising past their shoulders.

With a groan, Vera lurched forward and grabbed the stranger by the wrist. "Now!" she yelled, turning back toward Emaline.

Emaline tugged on the rope, helping pull Vera and the stranger out of the quicksand as they gradually trudged toward her. Once they reached dry, solid ground, the two of them collapsed onto their knees, panting. The stranger caught their breath and turned toward Emaline and Vera, staring at them for a moment. All at once, like a scared animal cut free from a trap, the stranger sprung to their feet and darted across the sand.

"Well, I guess we're not getting a thank you." Vera sighed exhaustedly.

. . .

Sitting on the horizon was a square building built on wooden stilts with a rickety staircase leading to the door. A red neon sign spelling out *The Stinging Scorpion* hung above the entrance in large, cursive letters. It stood alone at the top of a dune, like a beacon to wayward travelers.

"You thirsty?" Vera teased, leaning on Emaline's shoulder.

"I could use a drink," Emaline said. They'd been trekking through the desert for days without passing through a single town, rationing what little water they had.

"Good, because this is the best bar in all of Epilogue," Vera said, leading her up the stairs.

The inside of the bar was dim and dank, with bone-colored wood walls. Large, pufferfish-like lanterns hung from the low ceiling, glowing orange, yellow, and pink hues. Skulls of strange animals were nailed into the walls, fairy lights weaving in and out of their hollow eyes. The air was thick with a sickeningly sweet, bitter smell like molasses.

As Emaline took in her surroundings, she spotted a familiar face. "Is that…?" She pointed to a hunched-over figure sitting by himself in the corner of the bar.

"Let's go say hello, shall we?" Vera said, weaving through the crowded tables. She walked up to the man's table and slammed her hands down on it, rattling his glass. "How's life been, Wylie?"

Wylie glared at her, drowning himself in a pint of golden-brown beer. He wiped the froth from his lips and slammed his head down on the table. "My gang left me," he whimpered. All of his cockiness had miraculously dissolved the second his lips had touched his glass.

"Oh, I'm sorry to hear that," Emaline said.

"Don't feel bad for him; he tried to kill us!" Vera snapped.

"Some Aquis official came and asked about you. When my gang found out I'd failed to best you *twice,* they said I was unfit to be their leader," Wylie grumbled.

"What are you doing west of the tracks?" Vera asked, taking a seat across from him, Emaline doing the same.

"I wasn't just kicked out of the gang—I was kicked out of Jackal territory altogether!"

"Here, I'll buy you another drink," Vera said, flagging down a waiter.

Wylie blinked. "Really?"

"It's a pity drink since I feel semi-responsible for the state you're in," Vera explained. "Emaline, do you want anything?" she added, turning toward her.

"Oh, no, I don't drink alcohol," Emaline said politely.

"Okay, then. Two butte beers, extra frothy, and a cactus juice, please," Vera told the waiter, who sauntered off toward the bar.

"How pathetic can I get?" Wylie sighed.

"It'll be okay," Emaline said, petting the top of his head.

Moments later, the waiter returned from the kitchen, sliding their drinks across the table.

Wylie caught his pint and chugged it in one go, his face reddening. "They can't kick me out. I founded the damn gang," he cried drunkenly.

"I didn't know that," Vera said, sipping from her glass.

"Yeah, we were just a bunch of street rats with nothing to do," Wylie explained. "A lot of us didn't have families, so I thought we'd make our own. We were just kids back then, so we were looked down on, but once we were a gang, no one dared to mess with us."

"If I didn't know you better, I would say that your actions were almost noble, Wylie," Vera chuckled.

"Now, my gang wants nothing to do with me." Wylie sighed, tapping his finger on the side of his glass.

"You know, your gang might respect you more if you weren't going around shoving old ladies and trying to kidnap girls. I haven't forgotten about that, by the way," Emaline said.

"Out here, it's survival of the fittest. That's just the way things are."

"But it doesn't have to be. Vera and I have been going around helping whoever we can, and it's partly why we've been able to survive out here as long as we have," Emaline explained.

"Save your two-bit wisdom for somebody else," Wylie grumbled.

Emaline's eyes wandered down to the pair of orange goggles strapped to his hip. His boots were caked with dried mud, which had left a pile of gray powder on the floor.

"You're the guy we saved from drowning in quicksand the other day!" Emaline gasped.

Wylie's pale, freckled face flushed pink with embarrassment. "No, I'm not. You must have me confused for someone else," he said, crossing his arms.

"It's no use, Wylie. We know it was you," Vera said. "You know, you could have at least given us a thank you. Because of you I had to eat a cold breakfast."

"Listen, I'm sorry for running away, okay?" Wylie snapped. "I thought you two might still be angry and beat me up the second you got the chance."

"Oh, we're still angry. But we're also civil," Vera said.

"Well, thank you for, you know, saving my life," Wylie mumbled. "I owe you one."

"You could repay us by not ransacking poor towns with nothing to give."

"Listen, I'm a jackal, a scavenger. I take what I can to survive."

"I've always wanted to ask, but why jackals?" Vera chimed in.

"They're known for their cackle, and we like to laugh in the face of authority. We bow down to no one, not even those cultish freaks in Aquis."

"But aren't you doing exactly what Aquis does? Taking from people who can barely defend themselves?" Emaline asked.

"Don't compare us to those—"

"When I first met you, you were trying to drain a town's well. Do you know who started that little trend?"

Wylie went to speak, but found he had nothing to say. He had no excuse, no witty comeback to refute Emaline's claim.

"I can't imagine what it must have been like trying to survive in the city all by yourself. But you were able to find people like you and inspire them to be more than what society had decided they were. There are still a lot of people out there who are suffering, abandoned children just like you and your friends. If you really wanted to stick it to the man, you'd empower those people to fight back like how you did back in the city."

Wylie blushed, not from the alcohol in his hand but from Emaline's words. He shrunk back into his seat and sighed. "Maybe you're right," he said. Wylie stood on his chair and planted his boot onto the table, holding his finger up toward the sky. "I've decided, then! I'm going to *demand* my gang take me back as their leader. And once I'm reinstated, I'm going to start changing the way things have been run."

"He doesn't need much persuasion, does he?" Vera whispered to Emaline.

Suddenly, a man slammed his pint down into the middle of their table. He had a bushy, brown beard and a scar carved through his left eye. A tattoo of the deity Altera was engraved on the top of his bald head: a koi fish with two tails.

"I know you…" the man murmured, glaring at Vera.

Emaline studied the sudden tension on Vera's face, a fear that she had never seen there before.

"Oh, I must just be drunk," the man sighed.

"He's with Aquis, isn't he? Should we…?" Emaline whispered worriedly to Vera.

"What are you whisperin' 'bout?" the man growled, grabbing Emaline by the arm.

Still posing on the table, Wylie kicked his pint straight into the man's face, audibly breaking his nose. The man teetered a moment, then fell hard against the ground, unconscious. The pint crashed next to him, shattering across the floor.

"Don't mess with my friends," Wylie said triumphantly.

"Since when are we friends? I bought you *one* drink," Vera said angrily.

Wylie reached across the table and grasped Emaline's hands in his own. "Thank you, Emaline. It *does* feel better to be kind."

"I think you might still need a few lessons on what being kind actually means. But, nonetheless, thank you for the rescue," Emaline sighed.

A low murmur began to fall across the bar. Everyone's eyes had suddenly turned toward them and the unconscious man.

"Did they just knock out an Aquis official?"

"They must be troublemakers."

"That'll be bad for business."

Vera rose steadily and finished the last sip of her beer. "Let's go. We're not wanted here," she said.

Emaline and Wylie followed her out the double doors and into the blazing desert sun.

"I'm sorry for how I acted before," Wylie said, his voice more genuine than Emaline had ever heard it. "I just have a reputation to uphold. But I guess if I'm going to have a reputation, it might as well be a good one."

"I'm glad to hear that," Emaline said.

"Here, I want you to have this," Wylie said, digging for something in his pants pocket.

"What is it?" Emaline asked.

Wylie placed a gold keychain shaped like a laughing jackal in her hand. "It's something that I give all of my members," he explained, holding up his own. "Think of it as a token of gratitude for helping me find my way."

Emaline smiled, pocketing the toy.

She and Vera stood side by side and watched as Wylie got onto his hoverbike, driving off over the dunes.

"He's not so bad once you get to know him a bit," Emaline
said.

Chapter Ten

Two days after they left the Stinging Scorpion, Vera and Emaline stumbled across a river of half-buried cars. The cars' flat metal backs peeked out of the sand like stepping stones in a vast yellow ocean. Vera and Emaline walked above where the road once was, watching as a clay village began to rise up from the horizon, lit faintly by the dying red sun.

"Finally. It's been ages since we've been in a proper town," Emaline said, running ahead.

Vera caught her by the back of her blouse, holding her back. "We might want to skip this one."

"Why? Don't tell me you've stirred up some trouble of your own," Emaline teased.

"Because everyone in that village is dead."

"W-what?" Emaline stuttered.

"I came past here once," Vera sighed. "Trust me; it's not a pretty sight."

"But how did they…?"

"There's no well here. If you dig into the sand, you just end up hitting concrete. So, this village depended on Aquis instead. But in return, Aquis asked that the village give up its children to be initiated as new members. The village refused. Aquis took the children anyway…and then left," Vera explained.

"That's horrible," Emaline murmured.

"But that's not the full story, is it?" a loud voice echoed on the breeze.

They both turned and saw a woman riding a sepequs toward them out of the village. Yol and the man from the Stinging Scorpion rode beside her, sitting atop their own separate sepequs. The woman was burly and boorish, with messy eyeliner and a bright-red lip. She had on a black jumpsuit with two crisscrossing belts strapped across her broad waist. Her scar was jagged, cutting across her eye in a lightning bolt pattern.

"Run," Vera said.

Emaline stared at her, hesitating.

"*Run!*" Vera barked.

Emaline darted through the sand, pumping her short legs.

The woman laughed, swinging a long chain through the air and tossing it like a lasso. The chain wrapped itself around Emaline's legs, tripping her.

"Your fight's with me, not with her," Vera said, walking toward the woman.

"She threatened a high-ranking member of Aquis. That's cause for extermination," the woman said.

Vera snarled, her eyes burning with loathing.

The woman simply smirked, looking past her to Emaline. "Has she told you yet?"

"Emaline, don't listen—" Vera began.

"She hasn't!" the woman cackled. "This is *too* good."

"Told me what?" Emaline asked, sitting up, her legs still immobilized by the heavy chains.

"Your friend here used to be one of us." The woman chuckled, sliding off her sepequs. "She came from this village and was brought into Aquis's loving arms, just like me."

Emaline felt her heartbeat slow to a heavy drumbeat as if it wanted to stop altogether. Vera shot her a devastated look. She tried to talk, to explain, but couldn't form the right words, no matter how hard she tried.

"Did you know she was on her way to becoming an official? But then, the night of the ceremony, she got cold feet and ran away," the woman explained to Emaline. Her amber eyes turned back toward Vera, her grin widening. "We've been hunting you down for quite some time now. Unfortunately, younger members like Yol don't know what you look like. But when he gave me your description, I knew it had to be you. And after your little incident at the Stinging Scorpion, we've been hot on your trail."

"You remember me, don't you?" the man from the bar laughed. A bandage was taped across his crooked nose. "Your old friend Bram? I knew I recognized you from somewhere."

Silently, Vera slipped her gun from its holster and shot through the metal chains wrapped around Emaline's legs. Emaline squirmed free, unsure whether to stay or flee.

"You were always a fighter. That's what I liked about you," the woman teased.

Vera charged, rushing in front of the woman with her pistol drawn high. Before she could take the shot, the woman pulled a spiked mace from her belt and smacked it into Vera's side with a sickening crack. Vera gritted her teeth and tried to steady her aim, but the woman landed another blow against her shoulder, knocking the pistol loose.

"Stop," Emaline muttered, shaking.

Vera stumbled, cradling her ribs, blood dripping from her open mouth.

The woman laughed, raising the mace into the air above Vera's dropped head.

"Stop!" Emaline screamed, darting through the sand. She grasped the mace by the handle, stopping its momentum before it could deal the deadly blow.

The woman gazed down at Emaline with an emotionless, bored expression. But then something changed. A flicker of a smile spread across her face. "You know what? This is much better," she said, lowering the mace back into her belt. "Traitors deserve a slow death," she spat.

"Tilda, you can't be serious—" Bram began.

"Oh, I'm quite serious. It will give her plenty of time to repent for what she's done. I've already beaten her to the brink of death. Besides, there aren't any people around for miles." Her eyes flickered to the quiet, still village on the horizon. "At least not any live ones."

"What about her?" Yol asked, looking anxiously at Emaline.

"The girl?" Tilda laughed. "She's of no harm to us." The woman mounted her sepequs and steered it back around. "Come on, let's ride."

Yol and Bram followed behind her, disappearing into the distant village.

Vera collapsed onto her knees and then fell to her side, staining the sand red.

"Vera!" Emaline cried, kneeling beside her. She whipped her head from side to side, straining for any sign of civilization. She bit the end of her skirt and ripped off a piece of fabric, creating a compress. "Please, someone help," she whimpered, pressing the bundle of cloth against the wound and feeling it soak with blood.

Just then, she felt a presence appear in front of her. She peered up and saw the twin coyotes from Havert's farm. Their yellow, diamond eyes began to glisten as darkness fell across the desert.

"Oh…hello." Emaline sniffed, unsure whether to be terrified or not.

One of the coyotes knelt and nuzzled Vera's body up onto its back, carrying her off into the distance.

"Wait—" Emaline began, but the second coyote had flung her upon its own back, walking in its twin's footprints.

Chapter Eleven

What remains of the Old World lies buried in the sand,
Ready to become forgotten,
Everyday items,
Turned to ancient relics,
The only difference is time.

. . .

The twin coyotes stopped in front of a small wooden cabin with a fenced-in porch. Potted cacti stood guard by the door beside an empty rocking chair. A bamboo wind chime sang in the breeze, announcing their arrival.

"Who is it?" someone barked, opening the front door. A person in a metal wheelchair rolled themself out onto the porch. Their short, frizzy hair was held back by a plaid bandana while a loose tank top hung off their frail shoulders. A pair of pink slippers were pulled on over their feet. "Oh, it's you two," they sighed, noticing the enormous coyotes at their door.

"Can you help my friend?" Emaline asked, sliding off the coyote's back.

"Ah, you must be the one who gave the twins those tasty lizards," the stranger said, itching their stubble.

"Are they yours?" Emaline asked.

"Nah, they just come and mooch off me when they're hungry. Guess they got a little too used to me feeding them. Recently, I fell ill and was bedridden for a good while. I could barely feed myself, let alone these two, so I appreciate you stepping in when you did."

"Yes, I was the one who helped them, but now I need you to help me," Emaline said frantically. "My friend is badly injured."

The stranger peered past her at Vera, who was still lying motionless across the other coyote's back. "Bring her in," the stranger sighed, rolling back into the cabin.

Gently, Emaline carried Vera inside, laying her on a nearby table. Vera's eyes were sealed shut, and her mouth mumbled meaningless words. Sweat had begun to blossom across her forehead and ran down her cheek.

"Can you help her?" Emaline asked.

"You're lucky I used to be a doctor," the stranger groaned, rolling up their sleeves. They began to grab gauze and bottled herbs from a nearby desk drawer. "This may take a while. Why don't you go and wait on the porch? Give your friend a little privacy."

"Okay…" Emaline said, unsure.

"Don't worry. I wasn't lying earlier; this used to be my job back in Taproot City," the stranger said. "I've taken on much worse cases than this and managed to get the patient through alright."

Emaline nodded, walking out onto the porch. She sat on the ramp, curling her knees up to her chest and burying her face between them. Something wet and cold pressed against her folded hands. She peered up and saw one of the coyote's shaggy faces staring back at her.

"Thank you for bringing us here," Emaline said quietly.

The coyote nuzzled her cheek, forcing its head down onto her lap. Emaline petted the space between its ears, feeling her anxiety lessen little by little.

. . .

"All done," the frizzy-haired stranger called from the doorway.

Emaline blinked open her eyes. She'd accidentally fallen asleep, wedged between the two coyotes' warm bodies. While she had slept, night had fallen. The lantern nailed to the cabin door glowed a faint, fiery orange against the desert's darkness.

"Is she alright?" Emaline asked, standing.

"She will be with enough time and rest," they answered.

"I really can't thank you enough…" Emaline began.

"Mx. Ula. Call me Mx. Ula," they said, smiling.

"May I see her?" Emaline asked.

"Be my guest." Mx. Ula held the door agape.

Emaline crept inside the cluttered cabin and sat beside the table. Vera's chest was wrapped in white bandages, her breathing slow and labored. Mx. Ula had made her comfortable, cushioned beneath a quilt with her head propped up on a pillow.

"I'll give you two some time to talk," Mx. Ula said, disappearing into their bedroom at the back of the cabin.

"Vera?" Emaline whispered gently, turning back toward the table.

Vera's eyes opened just wide enough for her to be able to see. She turned her head, and at the sight of Emaline, began to cry.

"Hey, it's okay," Emaline said hurriedly, wiping the tears away.

"I'm sorry…" Vera said hoarsely. "I didn't want to lie to you, but I thought that if you knew the truth, then—"

"We all have a past we're trying to escape," Emaline said. "I certainly know that I'm trying to get away from mine."

"If you're going to know the truth, then I want you to know the *full truth*."

"Save your strength—"

Vera gently took Emaline's hand into her own. "Please," she begged.

Emaline sat in the chair beside the table and nodded.

"When I was taken by Aquis, a man named Rift took me under his wing. He was an official, and was in charge of training the new recruits. I showed great promise, so when I turned seventeen, they started to make preparations for me to move rank. But before I could, I had to complete my first mission. We were sent to a town that hadn't paid their fees to drain their well. I hadn't been outside of Aquis's headquarters before, and when I saw the state of the world—what we were doing to it—I knew I couldn't stay," Vera explained.

She paused for a moment, glaring up at the stucco ceiling. "When you become an official, they take one of your eyes. It's supposed to be a symbol of your devotion to Aquis—'an eye to see this world and one to see into the Other.' There was a time when I longed for nothing more than to prove my loyalty, always admiring the officials' scars as they passed by. But when that dagger gleamed above me, I only felt the natural terror of a scared child. I fought back and managed to escape, but not unscathed," she said, touching the scar on her cheek.

"I was like this when I first left Aquis, half dead and taken in by a stranger." She chuckled weakly with a bittersweet smile. "He was an old man who kept me alive only to tell me off. He was a tailor, so after he sewed up my wounds, he sewed me my vest. He told me that even if I came from a tarnished home, I could shine as brilliantly as gold."

“Sounds like he’s a good man,” Emaline said.

“He *was*. He died sleeping in his armchair,” Vera muttered. “After I buried him, I went back to the village I’d been born in, hoping I’d see someone and *feel* something—anything. But I knew none of them, not even in my earliest memories.”

“I’ll find a way,” Emaline said, catching Vera by surprise. “I’ll bring water back to Epilogue so that no one will have to depend on Aquis again. I’ll bring back the plants and the animals, and then you’ll get to see a butterfly, a real one.”

Vera laughed. “I’d like that.” Her eyes gently batted closed as she finally succumbed to slumber.

Chapter Twelve

Vera was still asleep when Emaline woke. She took in the room around her, admiring the gentle sunlight coming in through the dusted windows.

"With her kind of wounds, she'll probably be passed out most of the day," Mx. Ula said, handing Emaline a plate of fried eggs and cherry tomatoes.

"Thank you," Emaline said. "Here, for all your help." She reached into her dress pocket and pulled out a handful of oreales.

"Keep your money. It's not like I have anywhere to go and spend it anyway."

"Then what if I spruced up a little? As a thank you," Emaline asked.

"Now *that* I wouldn't mind," Mx. Ula sighed. "My husband and I used to do the chores together. But since he passed, I haven't had the gumption."

Emaline found a broom in the closet and began to make her way through the cabin, dusting and organizing. She scraped the grime from the windows, letting the sunlight spread across the walls and floor. Mx. Ula would check in often, always offering a cool glass of cactus juice and a plate of small brown biscuits.

"Did you know that doctors have to help *everyone*?" Mx. Ula asked while Emaline was sweeping off the porch.

The coyotes paced nearby, shyly peering at Emaline from afar before slinking away.

"That means that we have to help the guy who was stabbed *and* the guy who stabbed him if they both end up injured."

"That can't be easy," Emaline chuckled.

"Bad people, people who deserved it, people who did it knowingly—we still have to help them. Anyone who passed through those doors was a patient, no matter what they had done," Mx. Ula explained. "But I wonder if we'll be treated with as much compassion."

Emaline paused mid-sweep and tilted her head at them, unsure what they meant.

"Earth didn't become Epilogue because of some strange phenomenon. People knew what they were doing. We gave into every sin we have, and now we're paying for it. But even so, I wonder if whatever's out there, whatever's beyond all of this—if it's looking at us with profound disgust or profound sympathy. If it's thinking 'you're human' or 'you're *only* human.' You know?"

Emaline digested their words, looking into the vast blue sky and moseying clouds. "I'm not sure," she murmured. "We made a mistake, and there's no saying we're not to blame, but we can learn from it, can't we?"

"Perhaps," Mx. Ula muttered, pulling out a pipe and lighting it. "Bad habits are hard to break."

A heavy thud came from inside, startling them both.

Vera came limping out of the door, cradling her side.

"What are you doing out of bed?" Emaline gasped, rushing to her.

"We're sitting ducks if we stay here," Vera breathed heavily. "Aquis will figure out I'm alive sooner or later, and I'd rather it be later."

"Well, we can't go anywhere until you're healed, so get back to bed," Emaline said sternly, aiding Vera back inside. After getting Vera settled back into bed, Emaline walked out onto the porch.

"Iron will, that one," Mx. Ula laughed, chewing on the end of their pipe.

"I'd just call her stubborn," Emaline sighed, picking up her broom again.

"But stronger is the one who can stand up to an iron will," Mx. Ula said with a sly smile.

"I don't think I'm that strong," Emaline said, gripping the broom handle. "She's only in this state because of me—because I was too weak to do anything."

"People fight in a lot of different ways." Mx. Ula blew a ring of purple smoke. "Some use their fists, others their art or their words, but most rarely, some fight with their heart."

Emaline nodded, giving them a thankful smile before it fell back to a frown. Silently, she resumed sweeping the sand off the porch.

. . .

Emaline was washing dishes in the kitchenette's shallow sink at the back of the living room, gazing through the window out across the barren backyard. As she placed the last plate onto the drying rack, Mx. Ula rolled up beside her.

"You have an urn necklace," they commented, pointing at the small silver vial.

"Oh, yes, it's—"

Mx. Ula reached beneath the top of their tank top and pulled out their own urn necklace. It was more worn than Emaline's, a faded, gilded gold.

"Whose…?" Emaline began to ask, drying off her hands.

"My husband," Mx. Ula said, staring tenderly down at the necklace.

"How did you…cope with it? The loss?" Emaline asked.

"Nothing is ever really gone. I was sad when he died, of course, but he's a part of everything now. Sometimes, I find him in the tomato garden, or up in the sky, or in a cup of tea. His body may belong to the earth, but he gave me his heart long ago," they explained. "You don't need someone to be happy. You can live a fulfilling life all by yourself. But the fact that we got to live our lives together—grow old together—I will always be grateful for that."

Emaline's gaze moved across the room to Vera's sleeping figure.

Mx. Ula followed her gaze and smirked mischievously. "I hate to ask since you've already done so much, but would you mind helping me with one last thing?"

"Not at all," Emaline said.

"Your friend's vest could use some mending. I would do it myself, but my fingers are a bit stiff," Mx. Ula explained.

"Oh, I've never sewn before," Emaline said, unsure.

"I'll walk you through it." Mx. Ula grabbed a red metal tin from the cabinet at their side. They popped it open, revealing a large spool of white thread and a single needle stuck in a tomato-shaped pin cushion.

Patiently, they talked Emaline through threading the needle and then making her first stitch. Emaline's movements were slow and unsure at first, but she quickly gained more speed and confidence.

"Look at you; you're like a little sewing machine," Mx. Ula laughed. "Here, let me put something on for you while you work." They groaned, wheeling themself across the room.

"Oh, do you have a radio?" Emaline asked. Her father had always had the radio on while they were working. And sometimes, if the moment was right, he'd spring up and start dancing, helping Emaline to her feet to join him.

"No, even better." Mx. Ula smiled, blowing the dust off an old record player in the corner of the room. They plucked a record from the pile lying on the floor and stared at it with a happy sigh. Tenderly, they placed the record through the silver stud on the machine. Emaline watched as Mx. Ula hovered the needle over the spinning grooves in the disk and then let it go. There was a series of sharp pops, and then a song began to play.

"I've never heard this one before," Emaline said.

"Old World music." Mx. Ula chuckled, leaning back in their wheelchair and tapping along to the melody.

. . .

A week passed, and with each new day, the pain in Vera's chest lessened little by little. One morning, alone, she unwrapped her bandages and found that her wounds had finally sealed. She found her vest, freshly washed and mended, waiting for her on the table.

"My vest looks good as new," she said, walking out to the porch. "I suppose I have you to thank for that." She turned and nodded at Mx. Ula, who was smoking their pipe.

"Wasn't me, dearie," Mx. Ula said.

Vera moved her gaze to Emaline who did a small, awkward wave.

"Oh. Thank you, Emaline," Vera said, blushing.

"Looks like you're almost back to normal," Emaline said.

"Suppose that means you two will be going soon." Mx. Ula sighed, wheeling themself toward the door. "I'll pack you some food for the road."

Vera watched as Mx. Ula disappeared into the kitchen and then sat beside Emaline on the porch ramp. "I wanted to thank you for bringing me here. You've saved my life quite a few times now."

"It's the least I could have done," Emaline said, frowning. "If I knew how to fight, then I could have—"

"Your kindness came back to you," Vera interrupted. "I'm alive right now because you chose not to fight."

"But—" Emaline protested.

"Listen, I can teach you some self-defense so you can hold your own, but don't feel like we have to fight in the same way."

"Mx. Ula told me something similar," Emaline muttered.

"Besides, how many times have we almost died on this trip? This just happened to be a particularly close call."

"I don't know what I was thinking, dragging you into all of this," Emaline groaned, hiding her face in her palms.

"Hey, don't get it twisted. I chose to come with you, remember? And I'm getting a pretty big paycheck for it."

Emaline laughed softly. "Of course."

Mx. Ula came back out onto the porch carrying a neatly tied bundle. "It's all your favorites—cheese Danishes, pickled cactus, some smoked rabbit," Mx. Ula said, listing the items on their fingers.

Emaline walked over and hugged them, kneeling beside their wheelchair. "Thank you," she said.

"You know…I always wanted children, but my husband and I got so busy with our lives that we sort of forgot to have them," Mx. Ula said. "As selfish as it sounds, having you here, I feel like I got to take a glimpse of what that life may have looked like."

"I lost my father not long ago, and my mother has always been distant. Lately, I've felt…lost. Like a wandering child looking for its home. But this week, it felt like I've had a parent again. I wish I could stay, but—"

"Go. Live your life. Live it well," Mx. Ula said.

Emaline waved back at the cabin as she wandered off past the dunes, Vera by her side. Mx. Ula waved from the porch, guarded by the pair of twin coyotes.

Chapter Thirteen

Emaline and Vera had gotten comfortable living in the cabin. They'd gotten used to having homemade meals and a fan to sit by, which made adjusting back to the desert all the more difficult. A week had passed since they'd parted with Mx. Ula, and each day seemed to grow hotter than the last.

Vera sat on an overturned drain pipe sticking up out of the earth, fanning herself with her hat. "I never get used to this heat, no matter how long I stay in it," she grumbled.

"Here." Emaline knelt beside her, taking a piece of cloth from her satchel; it was the same handkerchief Vera had tied around her hand at the Light Market.

"You kept that?" Vera asked.

"Well, sure. It was a nice gesture—even if we were arguing at the time." Emaline poured water from her canteen over the cloth. Shyly, she placed the cold, wet cloth against the back of Vera's neck.

"Thanks," Vera mumbled bashfully.

"How are your wounds?"

"I've survived worse." As she spoke, thunder began to grouse in the distance. "Good. Maybe we'll finally get some rain."

"No, this isn't good," Emaline said, standing.

"What? Afraid of a little thunder?"

"No, because if there's thunder, then that means we could have a sandstorm coming our way."

Vera looked cautiously at the darkening sky. "What makes you say that?"

"Thunderstorms create a lot of pressure, and when that pressure is released, it can cause strong wind currents," Emaline explained. "So if a strong enough gust of wind ripples across this desert, it's going to carry a lot of sand with it, and we don't want to be here if it does."

"Which means we have to find shelter. And fast. Luckily, I know just the place," Vera said, putting her hat back on her head.

. . .

Emaline gulped. "Well…that's haunting."

Rising out of the sand was a half-buried hospital with cracked concrete and broken windows.

"It's not ideal, but it will have to do," Vera grumbled, looking out over the desert. There was a tension in the air—an uneasy stir in the wind. "You were right about that thunder. Looks like a nasty storm is coming this way."

"I-I'm just not a fan of hospitals. All of the prodding and poking," Emaline muttered anxiously.

Suddenly, a ten-foot-high wave of orange sand began to rise up from the ground, hurtling toward them. Vera grabbed Emaline's hand and ran toward the dilapidated hospital. Although the entrance was buried deep beneath the ground, they were able to slip through one of its many hollow windows. They fell down into a tiled hallway where abandoned medical equipment was strewn about. The wave of sand rushed past the window, howling loudly.

"Let's find somewhere safe to hunker down for a while," Vera said, brushing off her clothes.

Emaline walked close to her, bumping their bodies together. Her eyes darted anxiously down each dark corridor they passed, her breathing quick, uneven.

"You *really* don't like hospitals, huh? I think you'd prefer to be out in that storm," Vera chuckled.

"I just…got sick a lot as a child," Emaline said. "Luckily, my illness got more manageable over time. Now, I hardly notice it. But my mother was always scared it'd come back, so she didn't let me outside much."

"I'm sorry," Vera said softly, hooking her arm around Emaline's. "We can leave as soon as the storm dies down."

They walked into a spacious room with a high ceiling decorated with a dangling metal mobile. Couches were scattered about next to pots that once held plants. Emaline and Vera sat side by side on one of the sideways sofas, listening to the sand wash over the side of the building.

"I actually became interested in science because of my illness," Emaline continued their conversation. "I saw what medicine was able to do, not only for myself but for lots of people with all sorts of ailments. I wanted to use science to help people as it had helped me." Emaline's soft voice echoed through the dim, cool space, Vera heeding every word.

"My father had already been working on a way to bring the world back. He was overjoyed when I told him that I wanted to help. We took everything we did seriously, but at the same time, we couldn't help having fun. To us, it felt like a challenge, a puzzle we were trying to solve together. Whenever we pulled an all-nighter, my father would make me green tea to help keep me awake. He always knew just the right amount of honey to use…" She paused, rubbing the small silver urn between her fingers. "I just want to be a good daughter. He did so much for me; I want to be able to do this one thing for him."

Vera reached over, putting her hand on top of Emaline's. "You will. Even without my help, I have no doubt in my heart that you would make this journey no matter what." She paused, chewing her lip. "I've been meaning to ask, but what exactly do you plan on doing once our journey is over?"

"I'm not sure… I never thought that far ahead." Emaline admitted a bit sheepishly. "I guess I'll just go back home."

"It doesn't sound like that place was much of a home."

"It was when Dad was there."

"But now he's not," Vera said as gently as she could. "It just sounds to me like there's nothing left for you back there."

"But where else would I go?"

"There's a whole continent to explore!"

"Well, yes, but isn't it lonely, not having a home to return to?"

"Being the well-versed traveler that I am, I've come to realize a thing or two. One of the most important things I've learned is that home isn't a place, it's the people you choose to hold close. So if your family can't see the amazing person you are, then that's their loss. You deserve to be around people who make you feel loved–who make you feel at home."

"Thanks, Vera." Emaline smiled quietly to herself, staring half-lidded down at the floor. Her gaze moved across the room to the abandoned, rotting furniture surrounding them. Her father had always told her that memories were embedded in what the Old Ones had left behind, and if you were quiet enough, sometimes they'd tell you their stories.

. . .

Vera had been caught in a sandstorm once before and had had to wait it out huddled behind a canyon, wrapped in rags. She'd been bored to death then, but with Emaline, the time seemed to pass effortlessly. They talked for hours without even realizing that the storm had finally died down.

Vera stepped outside and took a deep breath, sucking in the humid air. The hospital had provided a moment to cool off, but she was ready to get back out into the sun. Together, she and Emaline walked alongside a series of telephone poles connected by sagging wires that hadn't pulsed with electricity in centuries.

"I just realized something," Vera said. "I told you what *I* miss about the Old World the most, but you never told me yours."

"Me? I'd say…trees," Emaline said.

"But we still have trees," Vera said, pointing to an ancient acacia.

"Yes, but there used to be billions of them, all sorts of species, and each completely unique." Emaline sighed wistfully. "I even heard that there were some places where the canopy would become so thick that you couldn't even see the sky."

"Sounds nice," Vera said, squinting up at the blazing sun.

Just then, a drumbeat began to play from behind a butte. Emaline and Vera both froze and listened to the upbeat melody. Curiously, they drew close to the butte, following the music to its source. They stumbled upon a group of women dressed in colorful robes, dancing around a raging bonfire. Two of the women were playing drums while another accompanied them on a wooden flute. The women's dancing shadows moved across the butte wall and along the desert sand, lit by the dying sunlight.

"Don't be afraid," the oldest of the women said, gesturing for Vera and Emaline to join them.

"What is this?" Vera asked, growing closer.

"A party. We're celebrating our freedom," the woman explained. "We came from a small village up north. There, we had no choice in when or to whom we were to be married. Our worth was only seen in our bodies and what our bodies may provide. We knew that we deserved more from life and from love. So, in the middle of the night, we snuck out of the village and have been traveling through this desert ever since."

"That's incredibly brave," Emaline said.

"It was necessary. Life in the desert isn't easy, but at least it's our own." She turned and faced Emaline with a warm, gentle smile, holding out her hand. "I'm Nyla," she said. She had sesame-colored skin, crow's feet engraved beside each of her slanted eyes. Her hair was brittle like straw and dusted with a layer of wind-blown sand.

"I'm Emaline. And my friend here is Vera," she said, shaking Nyla's hand.

"You're welcome to join in the festivities." Nyla nodded her head toward the fire.

"I don't really—" Vera began to say, but Emaline had already grabbed her hand and was dragging her away.

"Just follow my lead," Emaline said.

She stomped her feet to the beat of the drum, swaying her arms to the flute's melody. Vera awkwardly copied her movements, gaining more confidence as she went along. Their bodies began to move as one, waltzing and spinning together.

"You're really good at this," Vera chuckled.

"My dad taught me," Emaline hummed happily.

As the song reached its apex, Emaline bent back into a dip, kicking her leg up high, while Vera held her between the shoulders. Their eyes locked, glowing with firelight. Without missing a beat, the band changed to the next song, thundering down on the drums. Emaline and Vera retreated to the base of the butte, watching the flame from afar. Emaline studied the joy on the women's laughing faces, the freedom in their barefooted dancing.

Nyla walked over to them carrying two brittle pieces of bread. The bread was a flat disk shape, browned by the fire and seasoned with a sprinkle of turmeric. "Hungry? Sorry, it's not much."

"It's plenty. Thank you," Vera said.

Nyla nodded and wandered back closer to the fire.

"How close did you and your father actually get to reaching your goal?" Vera asked, chewing.

"A lot of people had been trying to find a solution long before we did. Besides being a scientist, my father was also an archaeologist. During his expeditions, he unburied old technology, blueprints, notes—anything about how to put the world back together again. We used them as a sort of launching point to make our own equipment. We invented some prototypes and ran some tests, but we were still in the early stages of development." She brought her knees up to her chest and rested her head on them, looking up at Vera. "If we're asking questions…could you tell me what it was like living in Aquis? Of course, I would understand if you don't want to—"

"No, it's fine," Vera said. "It was nice at first. I got warm meals and my own room. I was close with some of the other kids—Bram and Tilda, mostly. You wouldn't believe it even if you saw it, Emaline. They have a palace hidden out in the desert, with fountains of gurgling white water and pools that fill entire rooms and smell of lavender. There's enough to share with all of Epilogue, but they give us a fraction and keep the rest for themselves," she explained. "I really thought that Aquis had built a utopia. But as time went on, I started to see the cracks in their perfect palace. I did some digging into their records and found out how I'd ended up there. Then, after seeing what they were capable of with my own eyes…well, you know the rest."

Emaline wrapped her fingers around Vera's hand, squeezing it comfortingly. "You didn't choose to be one of them," she said. "And when you were given the choice, you chose to become something better."

"People need something to believe in, to make sense of things, and a lot of people find that within Aquis. A lot of them aren't bad people, not in their core, just misguided," Vera explained. "It started off noble enough, but somewhere down the line, they turned their belief into something else."

"Do you know how Aquis began?"

"People didn't always worship water—not until it became scarce. The idea was that water had an essence, an entity known as Altera. 'People had betrayed the water's gift, and Altera's rath scorched the earth and sky.' It was believed that if people dedicated themselves to the ways of the water, that Altera would bless them. Originally, Aquis helped keep the wells from running dry and brought water to struggling towns, but then something changed. Instead of handing out their 'blessing' for free, they started asking for fees. A little after that, the scarring rituals began, and a hierarchy formed. Eventually, someone proposed that if a town couldn't pay, then their well should be drained," Vera said. "After The Fall, Aquis took advantage of humanity's weakened state, and went across Epilogue gathering up all the water they could find. They hauled it out to their palace out in the desert, where they guard it with their lives—"

Suddenly, a guttural whooping came from the top of the canyon. The music and dancing stopped as the women all looked for the sound's source.

A muscular man with a single braid in his hair leaped down from a perch in the butte, two others following close behind. Colorful tattoos were engraved onto every inch of his pale skin, even drawn across the space between his narrowed eyes.

"Derex," Nyla muttered in terror, standing.

"Lost from your flock, little sheep?" the man asked loudly. "Come now, let's get you all back home."

Nyla pulled a spear from the wrap across her back and held it toward the man. The spear had an electrified, cylindrical tip with a long metal base. "I will never be your bride," she spat. "And these girls will never return to that horrid place."

"I don't think you understand… You don't have a choice in the matter," Derex snarled, taking out his own electrified spear.

A bullet shot through the middle of his spear, splitting it in half.

Vera stood a few feet away, her pistol drawn. "I'll give you a choice right now. Either you and your friends hightail it out of here, or next time, my aim won't be so poor," she warned.

Derex growled, yanking Nyla's spear from her hands and thrusting it into her side with a violent crackle of electricity. Nyla stumbled backward, collapsing onto the sand, groaning. Derex walked over to her and held the spear against her throat, the electricity tickling her skin.

She glared up at him, breathing heavily. "You call this love?" she spat.

"This isn't about love. This is about the future of humanity—" Derex began.

While he was still talking, Emaline tapped him on the shoulder. He turned and stared down at her with a perplexed look. She was tinkering with the device that'd fallen off the tip of his broken spear, rewiring it with her fingers.

"What do you want, little girl?" Derex growled.

"I'm not a little girl," Emaline said, pushing a button on the side of the device and tossing it toward him. "I'm a scientist."

The device burst with electricity, sending a shock through Derex's entire body. He stumbled backward, steam trailing off his figure. Groaning, he rubbed the static from his arms. "I'll get you for that. I'll—" He roared, charging for Emaline.

Before he could reach her, the other women linked arms and created a barrier in front of her.

"You'll have to go through us first!" one of them yelled back.

"*All* of us," another added.

Derex bit his lip so hard that an iron tang filled his mouth. He kicked at the sand and sighed, relaxing his fists at his side. "Let's go," he ordered his men, retreating back over the butte.

The women let out a cry of victory, hugging Emaline from all sides. But amongst their laughter was a hoarse coughing. Everyone turned and looked down at Nyla, who was still lying in the sand. Blood trickled down her mouth, glimmering in the moonlight.

"Nyla!" Emaline cried.

The women all gathered and knelt by her side. Vera lifted Nyla's robe, revealing charred skin, and then hurriedly hid it away.

"We know a healer. They're far from here, but if we hurry—" Emaline began.

"No…there's no time." Nyla coughed weakly. "I am glad that I got to reclaim my life, even if it was at the end of it…"

Her eyes gently closed as the breath left her body.

The women held onto one another's shoulders, bowing their heads in prayer. Their tears fell against the pale sand and down into the sediment below. Together, they dug a hole through the night and buried Nyla by dawn.

Chapter Fourteen

Emaline walked ahead of Vera, a heaviness in her footsteps. Half the day had passed since they'd parted with Nyla's tribe. The image of Nyla's makeshift grave weighed heavy on Emaline's mind. They'd only had a rock to use as the headstone; if any traveler happened across it, they wouldn't be able to separate it from the rest of the landscape. It wasn't the grave Nyla deserved; Emaline knew as much, even after the small time they'd spent together.

"Is everything alright?" Vera asked, matching her pace.

"I've just—I'm still not used to seeing—"

"Someone die?" Vera finished for her. "I've seen so much death, it feels sort of numb now."

"How could they do that to her? To all of them?" Emaline muttered. "If the Old Ones could see what we've become…"

"Emaline, it's always been like this. The world is in this state *because* of them, and now we're just continuing what they started—marching toward the end of the road with our heads held high."

"No, we can be better."

"And what if we can't?"

"Do you always have to be so cynical?"

"I'm just telling you how it is. You grew up in a perfect little palace where they taught you that you can solve everything with love. Well, you can't. Out here, love is what gets you stabbed in the back and left to die. And the quicker you realize that, the easier things will be—"

"But it's not true. You've seen it. The people out here, they're—"

"How long is it going to take you to finally *grow up* and accept the way things are?" Vera snarled.

Emaline flinched away, staring back at her fearfully.

Suddenly, the earth erupted with a deafening roar. An enormous sand flea burst from the ground, standing over thirty feet tall. It had a long face and an armored back, with a thousand flailing limbs. Before either of them could react, the flea crashed back down into the sand, swallowing Emaline and Vera whole. Emaline tumbled down the creature's throat along with a wave of sand, the razor-sharp barbs lining its esophagus slicing at her skin. She collapsed into a dry, fleshy chamber that swelled and contracted with the insect's breath.

Shakily, she propped herself up onto her elbows, taking in her new surroundings. Thin, stinging wounds were cut across her arms and along her face. With a wince, she got to her feet, dusting the sand from her skirt. Her eyes moved across the ground and spotted Vera lying motionless a few feet away.

"Vera!" Emaline cried, kneeling beside her. "Please be okay, please be okay," she repeated, gently shaking her by the shoulders.

Vera slowly blinked open her eyes, sitting up with a groan.

"Hurry, we have to find a way out of here before we reach this thing's stomach," Emaline said, standing.

"What's the use?" Vera muttered.

Emaline wrinkled her nose angrily. "You're giving up? Just like that?"

Vera pouted in frustration, turning away.

"You said that you never break promises."

"Yeah? Well, I changed my mind. I can't come with you to Jungo. Not anymore," Vera spat. "Do you remember when we were by the fire, and I said everyone needs something to believe in? Well, I don't know what that means to me anymore. I used to find it in Aquis until I learned everything they were was a lie. And now…I have nothing." Vera curled into herself, bringing her knees up to her chest and wrapping her arms over her head. "Sometimes I get this feeling…deep down in my soul…like everyone is bad, and the world is bad, and there's nothing any of us can do about it."

Emaline sighed away her anger, kneeling in front of Vera. "Do you want to know what my belief is?" she asked. "It's *people*, Vera. And every day, that faith is challenged, swayed by whoever I might meet, whether they be friends or foes. I always thought that people were good—that despite everything, humanity was *good*. But maybe you're right." Her head drooped over her chest, her hair falling over her eyes. "Maybe we're not worth saving."

Vera stared up at her in shock, the whites of her eyes like light glittering out from a dark eclipse. "No, don't say that. You don't really think that."

"But what if you're right? About everything? About Epilogue?" Emaline said, her voice quivering. "You've been out here longer than I have, you know better—"

Vera grabbed Emaline by the shoulders, shaking her head with a firm frown.

"Ema, If you'd asked me all of this when we'd first met, I would have told you a different story. But now I'm not so sure. While I've been showing you Epilogue, you've been showing it to me as well—a different side of it that I was too scared to explore before," she said, tears glittering in her eyes. "I think when I left Aquis, part of me…broke. But being with you, I feel whole again. I think that a lot of people in Epilogue feel broken…that they're searching for their lost pieces…and I think you might be the person to help them." Vera chewed her lip and averted her eyes, glaring down at the floor. "You have this…light in you. It's so bright and beautiful and it touches everyone that we meet. But I think being with someone like me would only dampen that light. Which is why I can't come with you to Jungo."

"But why? Why won't you let me—"

"Because I'm afraid," Vera cried, her voice cracking. "Because you make me want to believe in something again. And I don't think you understand how terrifying that is."

"The truth is…I know the world isn't a good place. I know that most people are selfish and that life is unfair, but I refuse to accept that that's all there is. We can't just ignore everything bad that's happening in the world, and we can't ignore the fact that there's still good in it either," Emaline explained. "I know that there are a lot of terrible people, but there are also a lot of people still here worth fighting for. And I'm going to fight for them the only way I know how." She held out her hand toward Vera. "Vee, you're amazing. If there's anything you should believe in, it's yourself. You have a good reason not to trust people and to think the way you do about things—but if the faith in yourself ever falters, if you want to trust someone again, if you want to believe in something again, then maybe you could start with me?"

Vera launched forward, wrapping Emaline in a hug. "Did you just call me Vee?" she teased.

"I'm pretty sure you called me Ema a little earlier," Emaline taunted back. "Oh, and I heard you when you called me 'princess' that night in Sundial."

Vera blushed bright pink. "You heard—"

Just then, a loud rumble rippled down the sand flea's body. Flashes of sunlight burst into the chamber as the flea roared, opening and closing its mouth from above. With one last great growl, the flea collapsed, and the chamber went quiet.

"What the hell was that?" Vera asked.

A blade stabbed through the flea's armored skin, sawing a square out of its flesh. The chamber wall peeled away with a string of slime, revealing the desert beyond. A woman walked into the chamber, wiping the slime off her thin, serrated sword. At the sight of Emaline and Vera, the woman perked up, lifting the goggles from her eyes.

"Kasumi?"

. . .

"What are you doing here?" Emaline asked excitedly, stepping back out into the desert sun.

"After we left the city, Hana and I came across some of the other vendors from the Light Market. They were inspired by you and wanted to fight back against Aquis, like us," Kasumi explained.

A band of people riding on sepequs were gathered by the base of the enormous sand flea, wearing layers of cloth and tinted goggles.

"Apparently, they thought my little speech to Yol was quite motivating," Kasumi added shyly. "So they sort of elected me to be their leader."

"And I couldn't be prouder!" Hana laughed loudly, walking up to them.

"*Sobo,*" Kasumi groaned, embarrassed.

"She's been doing a damn good job," Hana said. "Went from running a small stall in the Light Market to leading a rebellion."

"Well, I don't know about that. I'm still getting used to being in charge of so many people," Kasumi said, turning back toward Emaline and Vera.

"You know, I actually have a friend who could give you some advice on that," Emaline said, fiddling with the jackal keychain in her skirt pocket.

"So, what have you been up to since we last saw each other?" Vera asked.

"We've been helping deliver supplies to struggling towns and trying to keep the wells from running dry," Kasumi explained. "That's actually why we're out here. Sand swimmers like this big fella can feed a lot of people," she said, gesturing at the dead flea.

"We were getting ready to strike when we saw you two get gobbled up," Hana explained.

"We don't have much to offer, but you're welcome to camp with us tonight," Kasumi added.

"Hospitable as ever," Vera chuckled.

"I took your advice and started taking more confidence in my cooking," Hana laughed, patting Emaline on the back. "I'm the head chef of this little operation. My goal is to make a meal so good, even the Old Ones would be jealous of it!"

"Well, I can't wait to try it," Emaline said.

Kasumi led them down the dune, where the merchants had begun building bonfires. Chunks of the flea's flesh roasted above the fires on wooden spits, dripping with fat. Clay cups filled with cactus juice were passed around from a barrel tied to a sepequs's saddle.

"I had never seen someone talk back to an Aquis official like that before," one of the merchants said to Emaline, glowing with admiration. They were sitting across from one another, facing the fire. "No one has ever stood up to Aquis and lived to speak of it,"

Kasumi walked up behind him carrying a bowl of roasted insect meat and playfully slapped the back of his head.

"Well, except for Boss, of course," the merchant added with a chuckle.

"All of Sundial is in an uproar," Kasumi said. "Any official that enters the city has been met with an angry mob. The citizens are even starting to take back the water supply and tearing out the old pay pumps."

"I'm sure Aquis is thrilled about that," Vera sighed, sipping from her cup.

"I had no idea…" Emaline muttered.

"Word has it that the old Aquis head finally croaked, and one of his officials has taken his place," another merchant chimed in, sitting down beside the fire. "He'll have a hell of a time trying to get things back in order."

"Really? Did you catch who?" Vera asked.

"Fella by the name of Rift Krell, I think," the merchant said.

"I was afraid it would be him," Vera grumbled.

"Isn't he the one who took you in?" Emaline whispered behind her hand.

Vera nodded, taking an aggressive bite out of the bug skewer in her hand. "He's the worst kind of evil. There are some men who will admit to their own nature, no matter how cruel. As disgusting as they are, at least they're honest. But Rift is different. He kills and calls it mercy—looks upon his cruelty and calls it justice."

A heaviness fell over the camp, the merchants hanging their heads low, sharing anxious gazes. The fire crackled crisply, breaking the uneasy silence.

Kasumi stood and planted her hands on her hips, looking at Emaline. "You're still heading for Jungo, aren't you?" she asked.

"Yes," Emaline answered.

"I'd be wary if I were you. You've made yourself an enemy to Aquis and a symbol of hope to the people. From now on, all eyes will be on you."

Emaline nodded with a determined, firm frown.

"I wish we could help you more, but we've got our hands full." Kasumi sighed. "We're just a small few and the revolt is still in its infancy."

"Well, if you ever want more members, there's someone who may be willing to make an alliance," Emaline said, tossing her the laughing jackal keychain.

Kasumi caught it and turned it over in her palm, smirking.

"Their leader is a bit insufferable, but it sounds like you two have some common goals."

"You know what? I think I might just have a chat with Mr. Insufferable," Kasumi said, gripping the keychain tightly. "If we're exchanging gifts…" She tossed something to Emaline.

It was a charm the shape and size of a tea bag. The fabric was soft and crimson with golden thread.

“For good luck. I have a feeling you’ll need it.” Kasumi chuckled.

Emaline bounced the charm in her hand, feeling the weight of it sink into her palm. “What’s in there?” she asked curiously.

“A few spare oreales,” Kasumi laughed. “My grandmother always told me to keep a few on me in case of emergencies.”

Emaline smiled, tucking the lucky charm safely in her skirt pocket.

Chapter Fifteen

"There are plenty of dangers in the desert. Most people think the animals or the temperature is their greatest threat, but it's not. People are the thing you have to worry about," Vera explained. "That's why the best thing you can learn is how to defend yourself."

Emaline sat in the sand a few feet away, nodding and listening.

"Since Kasumi warned us that we might have some unwanted company coming our way, I thought this would be the best time to teach you some self-defense," Vera said. "Now, stand up and show me what you got." She got into a defensive position, holding her fists out in front of herself.

"What do you mean?" Emaline asked, standing.

"Try to attack me," Vera said.

"But what if I hurt you?"

"You won't."

Emaline threw a hesitant punch, which Vera easily blocked. While Emaline's hand was still extended, Vera grabbed hold of it and pulled her forward. She swung Emaline over her shoulder and tossed her against the ground. As Emaline's back hit the earth, the air shot out of her lungs in an audible wheeze. Her chest ached and her belly burned as her lungs tried to refill with air.

"You okay?" Vera asked, offering her hand.

"Yeah, just a bit winded," Emaline groaned, getting back to her feet.

"If you're able to knock the wind completely out of your opponent, then it's going to take them a moment to recover—usually enough time to make a quick escape," Vera explained.

"I may need more than a moment," Emaline wheezed.

"Well, unfortunately for you, we don't have a moment to spare," Vera said, smirking. "Now, try to swing me like I swung you."

"How? You're almost a foot taller than I am! Not to mention you're all muscle."

"Don't worry, I'll walk you through it." Vera winked.

She led Emaline through the motions, guiding her hands. Finally, after several tries, Emaline managed to clumsily swing Vera over her shoulder.

Vera gently hit the sand, laying on her back. "It's a start!" she laughed. Her laughter quieted as she spotted something off in the distance, squinting at it upside down.

"What's the matter?" Emaline asked, helping her stand back up.

Vera dug around in her satchel and pulled out a pair of binoculars, glaring through the infrared lenses. She watched as human-shaped blobs moved from miles away, glowing hues of red and yellow.

"It's an outpost," she muttered.

"Do you think they're friendly?"

"That's the part I can't figure out." Vera groaned, lowering her binoculars. "It would probably be best to keep our distance."

A loud whir began to echo from the distance. They both turned and saw a hoverbike flying over the sand toward them. The bike turned sideways a few feet away, skidding to a halt. The driver popped off his helmet as the bike lowered to the ground, its fans powering off. He was a brawny man with wide, muscular shoulders and a jawline carved out of marble. Gold gears were interwoven into his long, braided hair and a mechanical prosthetic sprouted from his right shoulder.

"Long time no see," he said with a toothy grin, stepping off his bike.

"Brutus," Vera said curtly, crossing her arms.

"Do you two…know each other?" Emaline asked curiously.

"You could say that," Brutus said with a wink.

Vera rolled her eyes. "We're exes," she explained.

Emaline blushed, staring at Brutus's physique.

"Do you have to sound so bitter about it?" Brutus asked.

"Did you forget the part where you took *our* bounty and left me to get caught?" Vera asked.

"Only after I learned you were going to do the same to me," Brutus protested. "We knew what we were signing up for when we got together. After all, a mercenary's first love is, and will always be, money. Speaking of, looks like you've found yourself a client with some cash," he said, peering at Emaline.

"Easiest job I ever took. I'm just taking her up to Jungo and getting paid a fortune for it. What about you? Have you come across any good bounties lately?" Vera asked.

"Actually, yes, I have," Brutus explained. "Heard a few promising rumors about a bounty out here in the sticks and decided to check it out."

"What kind of rumors?"

"You've probably already spotted that outpost—rumor has it that they're hoarding a very precious resource that would sell nicely at the Light Market," Brutus explained.

Vera cocked an eyebrow. "What kind of resource?"

"Oil," Brutus said with a mysterious grin. "Old World gasoline."

"Oil?" Vera repeated. "But how—"

"Not sure. But somehow, they figured out a way to make it."

"They must be keeping it to themselves until they can sell it to the highest bidder," Vera muttered, peering back at the outpost.

Brutus smirked. "Not unless we get to it first."

"We?"

"Yeah! One last job together; we split the profit fifty-fifty. What do you say?"

"Sounds like a deal." Vera shook his hand. "You don't mind, do you?" she asked, turning to Emaline.

"Ah, no, I suppose not," Emaline said, flustered.

"It shouldn't take long, and once we're done, it's just a skip to Jungo," Vera explained.

The three of them drew closer to the outpost, hiding between two dunes. The outpost was built into the side of a mesa and made of stacked wooden platforms. Vera zoomed in on the front entrance using her binoculars and spotted a small chamber dug into the mesa's rough rock.

"Looks like there are only two guards out front. The rest must be below ground," she muttered. "There's a makeshift elevator inside. We just have to figure out a way to distract the guards long enough to get to it."

"Leave that to me." Brutus swung his green backpack off his shoulder and rummaged through it, tossing out a random assortment of trinkets and tools. "Aha!" he yelled, taking out a small metal robot. It had a round body welded to a pair of blocky, spring-jointed legs. Its mouth was a crinkle of sharp, angry teeth with a pair of slanted eyes to match.

"Did you make that yourself?" Emaline asked, goggling at the robot.

"I did indeed, lil' lady," Brutus said.

He pressed a button on the back of the robot and tossed it across the sand. When it landed, it popped up onto its two little legs and waddled toward the guards, clapping its hands together like a children's wind-up toy.

One of the guards knelt in front of it, holding out his finger.

"What is it?" the other guard asked.

"I don't know…but it's sorta cute."

Just then, the robot sprang to life, latching onto the guard's finger with its pointed teeth. The guard yelped, darting back and forth, trying to pry the robot off. The other guard quickly left his post, attempting to help the other.

While they struggled against the robot's chopping teeth, Emaline, Brutus, and Vera snuck into the outpost. They came into a room of hollowed rock held up by wooden posts. Against the side of one of the walls was a rickety elevator. The three of them piled into the elevator, feeling their weight tug at the ropes keeping them suspended. Vera pulled down on the lever at her side, causing the elevator to slowly descend. The sound of grinding gears reverberated through the small, hollow space.

The elevator slowed to a stop in front of a chamber of carved stone, lit dimly by lanterns nailed into the walls. Up ahead was a tall metal pot filled with a boiling black liquid. People were gathered around the pot, mining loudly into the earth around it, hammering into the rock with pickaxes. Other workers in white lab coats were standing on ladders by the vat, pouring different vials into it like witches over a cauldron. A putrid smell hung thick in the air, attacking Emaline's senses.

"You might want to hang back," Vera whispered, drawing her pistol from its holster.

"You're not going to hurt them, are you?" Emaline asked worriedly.

"Course not," Vera said. "Just spook 'em so they'll hand over the oil."

Brutus and Vera stepped out into the light, cocking their guns in unison.

"We'll be taking that," Brutus said loudly.

The sound of cracking rock was silenced as the workers all turned and stared at them fearfully. The only noise left in the room was the bubbling of the oil.

"You've got some barrels over there. How about you start filling them up?" Vera said.

Reluctantly, the workers began to obey, turning a lever on the side of the vat and releasing the thick, black goop into one of the plastic barrels.

Emaline noticed a room hidden off to the side of the chamber. Tentatively, she walked into it and found a workbench pushed up against the wall. She scanned the blueprints and notes scattered across the workbench, lit by a candle melting in the corner. Her eyes fell upon a diagram of a bone. To an untrained eye, it may have looked like any common animal bone—but Emaline knew exactly which kind of animal it had come from.

"Stop!" Emaline yelled, racing back into the main chamber.

Vera and Brutus both looked back at her, keeping their guns drawn forward.

"I know how they made the oil," she said.

"Why does that matter?" Vera asked.

"Because it's made of *people*," Emaline said, trying to keep herself from trembling. "They're taking the bones of the Old Ones and melting them down to make fuel."

"But that can't be right. It takes millions of years for a fossil to form, let alone be used to make—" Vera argued.

"Exactly. This oil might look like the real deal, but it's not. It might as well just be mud."

"So, this liquid…it's all *people*?" Vera grimaced, staring horrified at the bubbling vat. She turned and looked at Brutus, expecting to see the same look of disgust, but saw only a content scowl. "You *knew*, didn't you?" she spat.

"Listen—" Brutus began.

"Anything for a quick buck!" Vera snapped, firing her gun at the vat. Bullet holes ripped through the metal tank, leaking the oil across the floor.

Vera grabbed Emaline's hand and raced her to the elevator, slamming down on the lever. The ropes hoisted them back up to the outpost's entrance with a noisy clatter.

"I'm sorry," Vera said. "I don't know why I thought—"

Emaline placed a caring hand on her shoulder and gave her a reassuring look.

"Thanks," Vera sighed.

"You two! Stop right there!" One of the guards from before came racing toward them. His fingers were wrapped in bandages, and what remained of Brutus's robot was scattered across the ground.

"Stay back; I'll handle this," Vera began. But Emaline rushed forward anyway, hooking her arms under the man's armpits and swinging him over her back. The air shot out of the man's lungs as his back hit the hard earth.

"You taught me self-defense for a reason, remember?" Emaline said, clapping the dust from her hands.

Vera nodded, impressed. "And it seems you took our lesson to heart."

The second guard rushed inside and froze when he saw his unconscious companion. Fearfully, he peered up at the two women and politely stepped out of their way.

Emaline and Vera were only a few feet away from the outpost when they heard a commotion behind them. The workers from the mine were flooding out of the elevator, coughing and yelling.

"Are they coming after us?" Emaline asked.

"No, it doesn't look like it," Vera said skeptically.

The last one to escape out of the elevator was Brutus, solemn-faced and serious. When he spotted Emaline and Vera, he trudged up to them, sheepishly rubbing the back of his neck. "You were right," he said. "Some things are worth more than money. That stuff may not have been real oil, but it was still flammable enough for me to start a fire. All their product, all their research will be ash in a few minutes. It won't stop them from trying again, but it will slow them down, at least." His gaze moved over Emaline, then back to Vera, a small smile creeping along his face. "I'm glad that after all this time, you've managed to find something worth more than any bounty. I hope that maybe someday, I can find that too," he said.

Vera's features softened, her lips curling up into a half-smile. "Me too."

☾ Chapter Sixteen ☽

Emaline fidgeted anxiously with her hands, glancing up at Vera every few seconds.

"What is it?" You look like you've wanted to say something for a while now," Vera said, keeping her gaze forward.

"So…you and Brutus were—"

"Whatever feelings I may have had for him are long gone," Vera said. "What about you? Have any exes wandering around somewhere?"

"There was a boy from town who'd have dinner with me and my family. I think my mom set the whole thing up. He confessed his feelings to me in the garden, but that's when I realized I didn't like boys." Emaline chuckled. "I take it you didn't have the same realization with Brutus?"

"No, I still definitely like guys…but girls are pretty too," Vera said, tipping her hat over her face.

"Do you…think I'm pretty?" Emaline asked.

Vera stumbled in the sand, tripping over her boots. She hurriedly regained herself and kept on walking. "I suppose so," she coughed.

"Well, I think you're pretty," Emaline said. "Though, you're also rather handsome in a feminine sort of way—am I making any sense?"

131

"I understand what you mean," Vera said. "Handsome, hmm? I like the sound of that."

Emaline walked to a cliffside overlooking an enormous crater with a small town nestled in its center. "There must have been a dam here once," she said, looking at the stone structures sticking out from the ring of sand.

"This should be our last stop before we reach Jungo," Vera sighed. "It's only a few more miles out into the Wastes."

"Why are they called that?" Emaline asked curiously.

"Cause that's what they are: nothing but desert. The entire continent is surrounded by an acidic, salt-water ocean. There's no reason to settle any colonies near it, so no one ever did."

"I've never seen the ocean before," Emaline murmured, touching her sea glass earrings.

"Eh, not much worth seeing." Vera shrugged. "The Old Ones left it in pretty bad shape."

"Just another thing to fix," Emaline sighed.

Vera glanced down at her anxiously. "You know…you don't have to feel responsible for the whole world," she said softly. "It's not yours to fix."

"I know that, but I want to. I have to *try*, at least," Emaline tried to explain.

"Well, just remember that you're not alone, okay?" Vera mumbled shyly.

"Vera…" Emaline began, the wind rippling through her hair.

Suddenly, the sand beneath her gave way, carrying her off down the steep slope. Vera leaped after her, sliding down the dam's wide curve. Emaline flung her arms out to the side, trying to keep her balance.

"Are you—" Vera began to ask.

"This is so much fun!" Emaline cried, laughing loudly. "It's like sledding!"

Their feet kicked up a rippling cloud of dust behind them as they slid down the steep slope into the village. The villagers' homes were concrete domes with hollow arched doors sealed by cloth curtains. The ground was rough and grainy beneath Emaline's feet, decorated with the fossils of small, aquatic creatures. The people of the village were busy at work, scraping a thick, moss-like algae from the walls. Some were drying the algae in the sun to be eaten, while others were weaving it into clothes on giant looms. A driftwood sign stood at the center of the town with the name "Muck" spelled out in seashells.

As they were walking, Vera spotted an androgynous child sitting alone by one of the domes. She knelt beside them and asked, "What's troubling you, friend?"

The child glared up at her and wrinkled their face. Their left shirt sleeve was empty, held shut by a clothespin. "I'm a runt," they said.

"Runt?" Vera chuckled.

"My brothers are all big and strong, but I'm small and—" The child glanced at their absent arm before glaring back at the ground.

"You look perfect to me," Vera said.

The child gleamed up at her a moment but then frowned. "Mama tells me that weak things can't survive out here. She says, 'You can't be a flower, you have to be a cactus.' That's the way of the desert."

"Look there," Vera said, pointing a few feet away. A bud had broken through a crack in the earth, spreading out its leaves toward the sun. "You see them everywhere. No matter how tough the ground gets, flowers still manage to bloom."

The child turned and stared down at the little bud in awe.

"A flower may look pretty and delicate, but they're just as tough as a cactus," Vera explained.

"I don't need to be a cactus. I'm going to grow up to be just as tough as a desert flower." the child yelled triumphantly, springing to their feet.

Vera took off her cowboy hat and placed it atop the child's soft, blond hair. "If you're gonna be tough, you gotta look tough." She winked.

The child glanced up at her and nodded, smiling brightly. Vera watched as they darted off into the village, laughing to themself.

Emaline bumped Vera in the side with her hip.

"What?" Vera asked.

"That was sweet. *You're* sweet."

"I just…have a soft spot when it comes to kids," Vera mumbled.

Together, they glanced up at the other side of the dome's steep slope.

Vera groaned. "I have a feeling getting back up will be harder than how we got down."

. . .

A few miles from the city built within the dam was a small rock quarry. As the sunlight retreated over the sand, Emaline and Vera pitched their tent in the center of the quarry, nestled within the rocks. The further they'd traveled into the Wastes, the quieter the nights had become.

Typically, the buzz of the insects and the howl of the coyotes was enough to keep Vera's nightmares at bay, but on those deathly silent nights, they ran rampant within her mind. She tossed and turned within the small tent, sweat glistening across her dark skin. Just as the terror within her swelled to its climax, she was shaken awake.

She sat upright with a loud gasp, finding Emaline sitting by her side.

"You were having a nightmare," Emaline said gently. "Was it about Aquis?"

Vera nodded. She reached up and ran the palm of her hands over the back of her shaven head. She could feel baby hairs beginning to grow beneath her fingers. "At the Aquis ceremony…I flinched away from the knife and ended up getting cut along the cheek. I fell and everyone started yelling, calling me a dissident. They wanted to hurt me—*kill* me. Rift had been the one with the blade. I thought he would understand, that he could help me. But when I turned around, he grabbed me by my hair and yanked me upright. He was going to toss me to them like a scrap of meat to a pack of starving dogs. So I took the knife from his hand and cut myself loose," Vera explained. "That's why I keep my hair short like this. When it starts to grow back, I get…anxious."

"I'm sorry, that sounds awful. I can give you a haircut in the morning, if you'd like." Emaline said. "But for now, you should try to sleep."

"I don't know if I want to fall asleep again," Vera admitted wearily.

Emaline reached over and pulled Vera close, letting her head fall onto her thigh.

"I'll stay with you until you fall asleep," Emaline mumbled with her eyes closed. "To make sure you don't have any more nightmares…"

. . .

Vera looked at herself in the cracked, handheld mirror Emaline was holding in front of her. They were sitting together outside of the tent, tufts of curly hair scattered by their feet. Vera ran her hands over her head, feeling its smoothness with a smile of satisfaction.

"How do you feel?" Emaline asked.

"Much better, thank you."

"I'm going to get a fire started so we can make breakfast," Emaline said, standing.

Vera stood beside her and took her hand, staring bashfully down at the ground. "I wanted to say sorry for what I said back when Nyla died. I didn't mean it," she said.

"I'm sorry too. I didn't say the kindest things to you either."

"If I'm being honest, you remind me of how I used to be back before I left Aquis—full of hope and optimism. And I guess I'm just scared that I'm going to see that hope leave you like it left me," Vera tried to explain.

Emaline cupped Vera's face between her palms. "It won't. No matter what happens, I'll fight to keep that hope alive…in the both of us."

Vera's face reddened and her eyes became lidded, determined. She began to lean closer to Emaline when someone yelled from the top of the rock quarry.

"Hey, lovebirds!"

Vera glared up the side of the rocky slope and spotted Tilda trudging toward them. Her sepequs slithered beside her, led by the reins in her hand.

"What do you want?" Vera asked.

"I went back to retrieve your corpse, but you weren't there," Tilda said.

"And now you've come to finish the job?"

"Oh, I would love to beat you a second time, but unfortunately, I have orders from the top preventing me from doing so."

"Orders? From who?"

"Rift, our new head. But don't get it twisted; he's not trying to protect you from us—he's just saving you all to himself. That's actually why I'm here. Rift was out looking for you when the Mitres declared him the new head, but he won't come back empty handed just because he got a promotion. I told him that I'd killed you, but he had his doubts. That's when he told me to stand down and head back—but you know me, never was good at taking orders," Tilda said with a smirk. "Listen, I'm not telling you all of this out of mercy. It's just that if anybody is going to get to kill you, then I want it to be me. Besides, if I killed you now, then Rift would kill me later. So I guess what I'm trying to say is…don't die, okay?"

"I won't."

"Do you remember when we'd sneak off after training?" Tilda asked. "We'd go down into the kitchens and steal as many dumplings as we could carry, then Rift would find us and tell us off, but he'd promise to not tell anyone as long as we shared some of our stash."

"I do remember that."

"You left us. You betrayed your friends—*your family*," Tilda snarled.

"I didn't have a choice. You saw what they did to those people…you saw what they did to *us*," Vera said, gesturing to her scar, then Tilda's. "I didn't want to leave you and the others behind, but if I hadn't left, I would have died."

As Vera drew close, Tilda's hands instinctively reached for her mace. But instead of an attack, she was met with a hug. Her fingers slipped down the mace, falling limp at her sides.

“I’m sorry,” Vera said, muffled into her shoulder.

“You can pay me back by not dying,” Tilda laughed, patting Vera on the back. She walked over to her sepequs and mounted onto the saddle. She gave Vera a small, thankful nod, which she returned. She whipped the reins and began to steer the sepequs back around.

“Oh, by the way,” she added, looking back over her shoulder. “When you finally face Rift, don’t look back on those fond memories. Because that man from your past, he’s not there anymore. So don’t go looking for him.”

Chapter Seventeen

Emaline couldn't believe it at first. Ahead of her, in the center of a ring of lush trees, was a pond. It was filled with blue-green water, lily pads sitting quietly on the surface.

Vera whistled. "That's a rarity if I've ever seen one. It's a miracle that any water can manage to survive this heat, all while avoiding Aquis's grasp."

Emaline walked over to the pond, kneeling on the pebbled shore. She stared down at her warped reflection in the rippling water, waving at herself. She dipped her palm beneath the water's cool surface, feeling a pleasant chill run up her arm. "It's mutualism at its finest," she said. "The trees create a canopy above the water so it won't evaporate, and in turn, the water nurtures the tree's roots."

Vera knelt beside her, dipping her hand into the water and linking it with Emaline's. She smiled at her shyly, then looked out across the pond. "Mutualism…that's the one where it's beneficial for both species, right?" she asked.

Emaline nodded, her eyes glued to their entwined hands beneath the water.

"I like to think that we've benefited from each other's company," Vera said shyly. "At least…I know I have."

Emaline twisted her hand away from Vera's and brought it up out of the water, drying it off on her skirt. "Well, I'm glad that you've enjoyed our time together, but I didn't promise you friendship, now did I? I promised you a fortune," Emaline said a little sadly. "We're close enough to Jungo by now. I'll transfer the funds from my account." Emaline dug through her satchel, pulling out a small, portable device with a pixelated screen. "What's your pin?"

Vera reached over and put her hand on the device, pushing it away. "It was never about the money, Princess," Vera said, caressing her cheek.

Simultaneously, they leaned into one another, locking lips. They parted, laughing, and kissed once more.

"You know, you remind me of a butterfly," Vera said, pressing their foreheads together.

"How so?" Emaline asked.

"You both bring me hope."

Emaline's eyes brimmed with tears, and her lips wrinkled up into a smile.

"Care for a swim?" Vera teased.

"Wha—"

Vera wrapped her arms around Emaline and pulled her down into the pond. They crashed onto a bed of lily pads, sinking into the refreshing water. Emaline popped to the surface, gasping for air from surprise. Vera emerged moments later, riddled with laughter.

"You!" Emaline yelled, playfully splashing Vera.

They spent the afternoon lounging in the pond and on the shore, eating the round, tart fruits growing from the trees. As the sun made its descent, they made a small fire and hung their wet clothes to dry on a nearby branch. They sat side by side, wrapped in the woven blanket.

"I'm glad Aquis didn't find this place," Emaline sighed, looking through the gaps in the canopy.

"Epilogue is a big place. Aquis may have taken most of the water, but they haven't gotten all of it."

"Just imagine…an entire world of this." Emaline gestured all around her, at the still water and rustling trees.

Suddenly, in the midst of a daydream, she realized something. "*Oh.*"

"What is it?" Vera asked.

"I just remembered that it's my birthday tomorrow," Emaline said. "I've been so busy lately that I almost forgot."

"What? Really?" Vera said. "How old are you turning?"

"Twenty-five."

"Ha! We're the same age. Though my birthday is in August, so technically, that makes me three months older," Vera said with a toothy grin. "I wish I had something to give you."

"Oh, please. Getting to Jungo will be gift enough." Emaline closed her eyes a moment, listening to the shifting of the water. "I can't believe our journey together is coming to an end."

"Well, you were the one who said that an end is never really the ending," Vera said, blushing from ear to ear. "This could be the beginning of something new…a *different* kind of journey…us, together—"

"Are you asking me to be your girlfriend?" Emaline teased.

"Y-yeah," Vera mumbled shyly.

Emaline leaned over and pecked her on the cheek, her touch like a prickle of glittering, warm light.

"I'd like that," she whispered softly.

. . .

Their clothes had dried by the next morning. They got dressed in the dusk sunlight, leaving the small oasis behind. They trekked over low hills of sand and dry, cracked earth until they finally arrived at a winding trench. Emaline stared at it from afar, miles of dug-in ground with grooves and imprints of where water had once been.

"The Jungo River," Emaline whispered. The breeze gently blew through her hair, cooling her hot skin.

"The name's a bit misleading, isn't it? It's not much of a river anymore," Vera chuckled.

"But it was once," Emaline murmured wistfully, imagining the raging rapids, the gurgle of the stream. She understood what her father meant when he had said it was the most beautiful place in Epilogue. Not because of what it was, but what it had been.

Slowly, she approached the edge of the river bend, unclipping her necklace and holding it out in front of her. "I've been carrying you with me all this time," she said. "You chose to use the last of your breath to tell me to bring you here, so I knew it must have been important. I owe you all that I am, and for that, I would trek a hundred deserts." She unscrewed the small cap at the top of the pendant and began to pour out its contents.

Gray ashes spilled out of the urn and fluttered off in the breeze, flowing down the ancient curves of the once-was river.

Thick tears rolled down Emaline's cheeks as she watched the ashes spread along the basin. "Goodbye," she said, waving weakly.

Vera hugged her from the side, offering her a shoulder to cry on.

As Emaline was wiping away the last of her tears, she felt something prod her foot from below. She took a step back, releasing a mailbox-shaped device which sprung up from the ground with a metal twang. It was a simple rectangular box with a small, oddly-shaped hole in the top. Emaline stared down at the device, perplexed. Her eyes wandered down to her pendant, which she hesitantly slipped down into the box's slot. It fit perfectly, turning into place with a satisfying click.

An artificial voice resonated out from the basin, "Welcome back, Dr. Gales."

The sand began to part at the bottom of the river, revealing a metal hatch leading down into darkness. Emaline and Vera turned to one another, sharing the same shocked expression. They reached out, interlocking their hands, and stepped toward the open hatch door.

The darkness felt endless. Emaline and Vera climbed down the cold metal rungs of the ladder until their feet finally touched a cement floor. Lights flickered on all around them, illuminating an enormous facility littered with science equipment. A desk with a square computer was pushed back against the wall next to a rusted facility sink. Emaline walked through the long facility, gazing at the rows of metal cabinets that lined the walls, each labeled in her father's handwriting.

"It can't be," she said, yanking open one of the cabinets and looking inside. She pulled out an air-tight, sealed package containing a single brown seed.

"Did your father ever tell you about any of this?" Vera asked.

"No, never," Emaline said, opening the neighboring cabinet and peering inside. "Vee, these are—they're—"

"What?" Vera asked.

"He did it," Emaline said.

"You mean he found a way to…"

"I think so," Emaline said, smiling ear to ear. That's when she spotted something on the desk pushed up against the opposite wall: a small present with colorful wrapping paper and ribbon. Tentatively, she walked toward it and turned it over in her hand.

Taped to the package was a note written by her father's hand. *Happy Birthday—Dad.*

Emaline tore off the wrapping paper with trembling fingers, letting it fall to the ground. Beneath the paper was a small white box with a thumb drive inside. Hurriedly, Emaline turned on the computer sitting on the desk and plugged in the thumb drive, feeling her heartbeat pulse in her throat.

A video popped up on the monitor, and Emaline hesitantly pressed play. And there he was. Emaline's father was smiling back at her from behind the screen.

"Hey, Sunbeam," her father said. "I assume if you're watching this, then I'm…no longer with you. I know you must have a million questions, but I'll try to answer them as best I can. I found this place during one of my expeditions, a lab left behind by the Old Ones. It was here that I discovered an unfinished machine—a last desperate attempt to reverse the damage that had been done to the world. I began to repair the device, but shortly in, I hit a roadblock in my work. That's when I realized that your designs, the theories that you had developed, were the last key in the puzzle. It was here that I turned your ideas into reality."

A light flashed on at the back of the facility, illuminating a tall, cylindrical device. It was made of white metal with black detailing, a single glowing red button staring back at Emaline from afar.

"I call it the God Finger," her father said, peering at where the device was. "It's filled with spores, a collection of vital flora engineered to withstand our new climate. There's also a condensed formula that, when activated, will create artificial clouds ripe with rain, ready to fertilize said spores. Essentially, with the press of that button, you will be able to bring life back to Epilogue. It won't reverse all of the damage we've done, but it'll be a good start."

Emaline stared at the machine, overwhelmed by the immense power stored within it.

"I'm sorry for keeping this a secret from you. Your mother always kept close ties with Aquis, and I feared what they'd do to you if they found out you'd been here working with me on this machine. I assumed that the less you knew, the better. If Aquis were to ever interrogate you, I wanted you to have no knowledge of this machine or its potential." He paused. "I was so excited when you asked me to be my lab partner, but I was also somewhat disturbed. You were only a child then, and it shouldn't be the burden of a child to fix the world. And even though it was not by my hands, I felt the guilt of those who had robbed their children of their future. So I worked on the machine in secret, hoping that one day I could give you a gift befitting of everything you've given me. But I guess, in the end, I needed your help anyway. A small part of the machine had wasted away with time, a vital mechanism to filtrate the solution."

Emaline gasped. "The water purifier."

"Yes," her father said, as if he'd heard her reaction. "Your little water purifier worked perfectly. There's a few other components of yours that I'm sure you'd recognize if given the chance to take the machine apart." He chuckled, smiling.

Her father paused for a moment, stroking his silver stubble while staring down at the floor. "I'm sorry. I shouldn't have let your mother keep you cooped up in that place. I thought it was for the best, that I was keeping you safe, but at what cost? I hoped that by asking you to bring my ashes here, you would finally get a chance to see the world, and decide your place within it," her father said softly, his eyes meeting hers. "I'm so proud of you for getting this far. I'm sure it couldn't have been easy. But I hope that this gift is well worth it. Remember, no matter how much time passes, no matter how you or the world may change, that your Papa loves you. Always.”

The video ended, freezing on Emaline’s father’s smiling face.

Emaline stumbled back from the desk, her entire body trembling. Vera caught her from behind before her legs could give out.

“I can’t believe he—he really—” she stammered.

Vera swung Emaline off her feet and spun her, laughing loudly. “You did!” she cried happily. “You brilliant woman, you did it!”

“Well, I mean, it was a co-effort,” Emaline protested, flustered.

“You heard the video for yourself! This wouldn’t have been possible without *your* ideas.” Vera gently lowered Emaline back to the ground and gazed back at the God Finger. “This is going to change everything.”

“Which is exactly why I can’t let you press that button,” a voice said from behind them, followed by the cocking of a gun.

Emaline and Vera whipped around, spotting a man at the back of the room. He was tall and lean with straight, pale-blond hair that draped down over his shoulders. He wore a hooded robe that shimmered like moonlight and was cinched at the waist by a silver cord. A necklace with Aquis’s symbol, the two-tailed koi fish, hung low against his chest. In one hand, he held a silver pistol, and in the other, a blackened dagger. A crisscrossed scar cut through his right, unseeing eye.

"It's been a long time," Vera said. "Heard you were promoted to Aquis head. Congratulations."

"News travels fast." Rift sighed, combing back his hair. "I've been bombarded with a sea of reports concerning you two—stirring up an uprising in Sundial, taming the Golden Jackals, even smashing a pint into Bram's poor face. I must admit, it's been quite entertaining. But when Tilda told me she'd finally bested you, I knew it couldn't have been the truth. You're like a bad memory—never really gone and always popping up at the most inconvenient times." His voice was gentle and cold, like a brisk wind.

"I could say the same about you," Vera spat. "If there's one thing we have in common, I think it's that neither of us enjoys idle chitchat." She slipped her pistol from its holster.

Rift smirked, lowering his gun while raising his dagger. He pointed the blade toward Vera, angling it at her eye from afar. "I always knew that one day, your flesh would finally feel my blade," he said. "Either branded as an official of Aquis or slain as one of its enemies."

In perfect unison, they drew their weapons and charged.

Chapter Eighteen

It is only

In this barren land

That the hearts of humanity

Can truly bloom.

. . .

Emaline had seen this all before. She had seen it when Vera fought off the coyotes at the farm, and then again with Tilda. That same horrible dread crept up her spine and turned her muscles to stone. Though she wanted to look away, her eyes were too scared to move, to blink, for fear of Vera no longer being there when she opened them next.

With incredible speed, Rift lunged toward Vera with his obsidian dagger. Before the blade could reach her, Vera smacked the dagger upward with the barrel of her pistol. While Rift staggered backward from the force, Vera released a warning shot, skimming his cheek.

The head official caught his fall, sliding his hand over the wound and rubbing the beads of blood between his fingers. "You're quick, I'll give you that," he spat. "But I'm quicker."

They fought beautifully, like two dancers, each move artistically calculated. The fight became a blur of blades and bullets until they finally leaped to opposite sides. They stared at each other, panting, bleeding.

"Emaline!" Vera yelled, her voice echoing down the long facility.

Emaline twitched, suddenly brought back to reality.

"I'll hold him off. Get to the God Finger and press the button," she continued, peering back over her shoulder with a toothy grin. "Go save the world for me."

Emaline nodded tearfully, darting down the corridor toward the looming machine.

"No!" Rift roared, slashing wildly at Vera, who blocked with the side of her gun.

"Isn't this what Altera would *want*?" Vera asked, wincing. "Water is a gift—a blessing from Altera to us here on Epilogue."

"That's what you never understood," Rift said, pausing his attack to wipe the sweat from his chin. "Only those who are *worthy* are deserving of that blessing."

"And what gives you the power to decide who is worthy and who isn't?" Vera snarled.

"Because *I* speak for Altera and its will." Rift smiled mysteriously.

Vera stood a moment, glaring hard at the ground. Suddenly, she whipped her pistol up toward the ceiling, its gold glimmering under the fluorescent lights. "You've never worshiped anything higher than yourself. Your words do not speak for Altera; they come from your own twisted mind. And if, somehow, they *do* truly speak for the water, then Altera has no home in my heart," Vera spoke loudly. She dropped her arm, holding her gun straight out in front of her. "Do you really think if it could see what you've turned into—what you've turned *it* into—that it would be proud?"

Rift tossed his dagger aside and mirrored Vera's stance, holding up his silver pistol. "Let's go ask it ourselves," he said coolly.

Two bullets whizzed through the air simultaneously, striking them each in the opposite shoulder. Blood speckled the concrete floors, running through their fingers as they each grasped at their wounds.

"You were always my star pupil…but there was one lesson you refused to learn," Rift snarled.

"And what would that be?" Vera asked, nursing her hurt shoulder.

"If you have the chance to kill, you take it." Rift aimed past Vera to Emaline.

"No!" Vera cried, shoving Rift's arm as he fired.

She turned and watched as the bullet hit Emaline in the side, knocking her down to the ground.

The God Finger was only a few feet away, raised up on a three-step pedestal. Emaline began to drag herself toward it with a pained groan.

While Vera stared in horror, Rift took the opportunity to grab his dagger. He sprung up from behind, slashing the blade across Vera's face. She stumbled and fell, her vision turning crimson.

"I told you you'd meet my dagger someday," Rift said coolly. As he went to walk away, he felt something grasp his ankle. He peered down at Vera's outstretched hand, her face flat against the ground next to a splatter of red.

"Don't…hurt her," she mumbled almost inaudibly.

"Oh, still conscious, are we?" Rift spat. "I've shot you in the shoulder and lacerated your face, and yet you cling to my ankle like a rabid dog just to protect her. And for what? Loyalty? Love? I taught you better than that." With one forceful step, he yanked her fingers loose and began to walk away.

With the last of her strength, Vera stretched her fingers helplessly toward him, but then fell limp against the ground.

Emaline crawled up the three steps leading to the God Finger, grasping for the red button. Just as her fingers grazed it, Rift rolled her onto her back using his foot. He pinned her to the steps, slamming the heel of his shoe down onto her stomach.

"Do you really think this is what Altera would want?" Emaline wheezed.

"You and Vera both! This was *never* about Altera!" Rift roared. "You're nothing but a little girl with naïve ideas. Let me tell you something: there is no such thing as hope. Not for us, anyway. Humanity's been on a trajectory for destruction ever since we first began. And now, we're almost at the end. I don't care about Aquis or its followers; I just want to help humanity finally *lay to rest.*" He lifted his shoe from her abdomen and knelt, leaning in close so that his lips skimmed her ear. "Deep down, don't you want to see it too? To let it all end—to finally close the book?" he whispered.

"No," Emaline said, surprised by her own answer.

Rift lifted his head, staring down at her curiously. "No?" he repeated.

"Because it's still good," she said softly. "Because if there is even one ounce of kindness, of beauty, of love left in this world, then I think it's one worth living in. I've seen it. Even on this dying planet, there are still people who want to help, who want to change, who have words and thoughts and feelings that matter—that are worth saving."

"You can't change human nature," Rift began, wrinkling his nose.

"Change *is* human nature," Emaline yelled. "And now, more than ever, we have the chance to change our story. We can change it with love!"

"Love, peace—those are nothing but the fleeting dreams of children," Rift spat.

Emaline rose up onto her feet and reached into her dress pocket, pulling out the lucky charm Kasumi had given her. The bullet had shot through its middle, half-embedded in the silver oreales held inside. "Love has saved me countless times—love is why I am still standing here!" Emaline yelled. "We can put things back together—the right way this time. But I can't do it alone," she said, holding out her hand.

Rift could have sworn that in her pupils, he caught a glimpse of a two-tailed fish, and it made him tremble. He stared at the gesture momentarily, his eyes flickering with desperation, a longing to reach out. But then the flicker faded and was replaced by a cruel glare. He whipped out his dagger and lunged forward, stabbing it through her hand.

Emaline's back smacked against the cold, hard metal of the God Finger machine. Rift glared down at her with a toothy grin, thrusting the knife deeper through her hand.

"Did you really think I'd switch sides after your pathetic little speech?" he taunted.

Emaline winced and smiled at the same time. "No, but I did think you'd stab me right where I wanted you to. Thanks, by the way," she said.

"For what?" Rift asked, amused.

"For pushing the button for me."

Rift's eyes widened, slowly moving down to his dagger. The blade had gone through Emaline's hand down into the hard plastic of the red button.

"No," he muttered, shaking his head. "No!" he yelled once more, yanking the dagger loose.

The God Finger whirred to life, shooting out steam from its base. With a mechanical shutter, it began to rise up toward the ceiling, which peeled open, letting in a puff of glittering sand. Emaline watched as the God Finger climbed higher and higher into the sky until it eventually stopped. With a deafening *boom*, a cloud of bright-green spores erupted from the tip of the finger, filling the sky. The explosion of life could be seen all over Epilogue as the spores began to fall over the desert.

Havert tilted his sunhat from his eyes, peering up at the sky with his daughter by his side.

Kasumi watched the explosion from atop a high mesa, Hana's hand on her shoulder.

Wylie stared from the hood of an old car in the scrapyard the Jackals called home.

At the bottom of a dam, a child looked up in awe.

All across Epilogue, every eye was set on the sky.

Rift dropped his dagger and pistol, letting them clatter to the floor. He stared, disheveled, at Emaline, who had her fist gripped at her side, dripping with blood.

"Excuse me," she said politely, sneaking past him. She wetted an old rag under the facility sink and walked over to Vera. She reached out, touching the top of Vera's head. At first, Vera flinched away, but quickly recognized Emaline's gentle caress and embraced it. Gingerly, Emaline wiped away the blood, revealing a long gash cut across Vera's forehead and over her nose. Vera blinked open her eyes, the pupils dancing at the sight of Emaline.

"Thank the stars, he missed your eyes," Emaline sighed with relief.

"Did we do it?" Vera asked weakly. "Did we save the world?"

Emaline nodded, holding back tears.

"I just have one question then…"

"What is it?" Emaline asked.

"Do you like women with scars?" Vera teased with a wink.

"How could you make a joke at a time like this?" Emaline laughed, letting her tears loose.

"Come on, Princess. Tell me, do you like 'em rugged?" Vera wrapped her arms around Emaline, who giggled loudly.

Rift stared from afar, shocked to silence. He watched as the two women tended to each other's wounds with a tenderness he had longed for his entire life—that he could scarcely believe existed. His life had been filled with cruelty. Any dream of love or peace had been beaten mercilessly out of his mind and body. His father, the Aquis head before him, had ensured that Rift would be just as cold and ruthless a leader as he had been. As Rift grew older, he came to loathe the human race, seeing the extent of its brutality. He knew humanity was already lying in its grave, but he wanted to be the one to hammer the final nail into the coffin. But now his heart beat unsurely.

He studied the smile on Vera's face. She had been his student. She had trusted him once. And now his hands were stained with her blood, her face permanently scarred by his dagger. The poison in his soul fought to break loose, to lash out, to rip apart the empathy he saw before him as he had been taught to do. But something held him back, a piece of himself he had lost long ago—a small boy who didn't like to see people get hurt.

If a tenderness like this could exist, he thought, then maybe the world and the people in it weren't all bad. But it wasn't all good either, he knew. It just was. And maybe he could learn to be content with that.

"There," Emaline sang, patching up the last of Vera's wounds. "Now all we have to worry about is—" She went to look at Rift, but he was no longer there. "Should we be concerned about that?"

"Don't worry," Vera reassured her, getting to her feet with a tired groan. "I'm sure this isn't the last we'll be seeing of him."

. . .

Emaline and Vera climbed back up the ladder and out into the desert. They walked side by side, hand in hand, as the sky darkened above them. Rain began to fall one droplet at a time, running down their faces and through their hair. The rain soaked into the sand, enriching the soil with nutrients.

"Everything is going to be different after this," Emaline muttered.

"Not everything," Vera said, squeezing her fingers. "So, what do we do now?"

Emaline turned and looked back at the metal hatch buried at the bottom of the basin. "The world isn't saved just because we pressed a button. There's still lots of work to be done. I don't know what we might encounter or where we may have to go, but I know that I want you there by my side. So, what do you say?" she asked.

Vera raised Emaline's hand to her lips and gently kissed her knuckles.

161

"Darling, I'd follow you to the end of the world and back."

162

To be continued...

9 781966 196242